Roger Ormerod lives in Wolverhampton, England, and is the author of more than thirty novels of suspense. He entered the Civil Service in 1937, serving ten years in the county courts. He has also worked as a Social Security inspector, postman and production control officer in a heavy industry factory. In recent years, he has devoted himself to his flourishing career as a novelist and to his photography and painting.

# PARTING SHOT

When Owen Tanner's Scandinavian wife Karin vanishes, he assumes that she has left him. But then his home is ransacked and he begins to wonder if he has jumped to the wrong conclusion. And when he receives a distressed call from Karin in Sweden, his suspicions are confirmed. Owen leaves immediately for Scandinavia, determined to find out the truth. During the crossing, he meets beautiful Finlander Eija Karlsson who seems keen to help him in his quest. Owen finds himself somehow caught up in the hunt for international diamond thieves. Finally, he uncovers a story behind his wife's departure that he could never have imagined . . .

*Books by Roger Ormerod*
*Published by The House of Ulverscroft:*

A GLIMPSE OF DEATH
TIME TO KILL
FULL FURY
A SPOONFUL OF LUGER
SEALED WITH A LOVING KILL
THE COLOUR OF FEAR
DOUBLE TAKE
A DIP INTO MURDER
THE WEIGHT OF EVIDENCE
ONE DEATHLESS HOUR
CART BEFORE THE HEARSE

# ROGER ORMEROD

# PARTING SHOT

*Complete and Unabridged*

## ULVERSCROFT
*Leicester*

First published in Great Britain in 1998 by
Severn House Publishers Limited
Surrey

First Large Print Edition
published 1999
by arrangement with
Severn House Publishers Limited
Surrey

British Library CIP Data

Ormerod, Roger, 1920 –
Parting shot.—Large print ed.—
Ulverscroft large print series: mystery
1. Suspense fiction
2. Large type books
I. Title
823.9′14 [F]

ISBN 0–7089–4126–5

LEICESTER CITY
LIBRARIES

0708941265 2 507

UWERS        15.9.99

F            £14.99

Published by
F. A. Thorpe (Publishing) Ltd.
Anstey, Leicestershire
Set by Words & Graphics Ltd.
Anstey, Leicestershire
Printed and bound in Great Britain by
T. J. International Ltd., Padstow, Cornwall

This book is printed on acid-free paper

To Signe and Kenneth Keys for their assistance with Swedish traditional costume, to Doris Ranft for her friendship, and especially to Eija Rantanen for 'I love you' in Finnish.

*Chastity*: Freedom from all unlawful commerce of sexes.

*The Student's English Dictionary*
Ogilvie & Annandale, 1895

# Prologue

The cobbles were still slicked with rain, though it had stopped early in the evening. Wind was rattling round the van. Across the end of the alleyway the few pedestrians had been walking head down, not to be diverted, but by midnight nothing was moving. The van sat, apparently empty, and now part of the scenery. Paper had blown beneath its wheels and become trapped. The engine was cold, and one tyre was at half pressure.

At ten minutes past midnight the rear doors of the van opened and two men quietly lowered themselves to the cobbles. They were dressed in running shoes, dark slacks and black roll-neck sweaters. The woman who slid forward over the bench seat was slim, her face pale, and had her hair tied back beneath a dark blue headscarf. In all other ways she was dressed the same as the two men. She took her seat behind the wheel. The men did not speak to her, but moved away into the darkness, disappearing into a narrow opening between the tall buildings.

She sat. She waited. There was no tension on her features, because this would not need

1

a fast getaway. The van had been chosen for its derelict and anonymous appearance, rather than for its speed.

Ten minutes later a dark green minivan drifted into the far end of the alleyway behind her. It lifted its wheels onto the pavement and nestled close into the shadows beneath the buildings. Its lights had been extinguished before it made the turn, and the woman did not notice it in the single rear-view mirror on the door of the van.

There was silence. A lone police patrol car drove past the far end of the alley, but without pause. The woman glanced at her watch, but the dial was not visible. She reached for a cigarette, then decided against it.

The two men had found the window. It had been left only fractionally open, and had been difficult to locate in the row of similar windows, some higher and some lower, all so deeply shadowed that it had required an overactivity of the torch to locate the correct one. Its use had probed at the nerves of the shorter of the men.

'There's got to be alarms.'

The taller one was all confidence. 'I told you,' he whispered. 'In these places the security's all for the daytime. They have to worry about armed idiots, when their

2

stuff's all out of the strongroom. At night the security's concentrated on the strongroom door. Relax, Niels, and I'll give you a shove up.'

Niels grumbled. The job was bigger than they'd ever tackled before. 'We left the gun in the car.'

'Guns! It's all you think about. This job's all technique. Quiet, Niels, not your bloody bangs in the night. Where's your foot?'

Then they were inside. This was the women's rest room. The taller one seemed to know his way around and located the door by touch. 'Alarms! You're crazy.'

They were in a narrow corridor, linoleum beneath their padding feet, and up the stairs ahead. The door at the top was locked. Urged by his brother's gloved hand, Niels moved forward. He had the slim crowbar ready, and the door flew open with a crack. They stood, their breathing quiet. Then Niels thrust open the door.

They were in the inner office used by Helen Strange, PA to the managing director of Hammerstein & Co, jewellery restorers. To their right, now dimly visible because a side window looked out on the street, there was a frosted glass door that opened into the reception office, to their left a similar door, with the plain inscription: J Hammerstein.

This door, too, was locked. Niels raised the crowbar to the glass, an abrupt, impatient gesture. His brother caught his arm and pointed to the jamb. Another brittle crack, and they were inside.

Two long windows, shades up, with the room brightly lit by streetlamps, a large, cleared mahogany desk, thick carpeting, a single phone — it was plain but impressive. Here, Jacob Hammerstein, leading restorer in Europe, interviewed his clients, relieved them of jewellery that had become sadly jaded after a dozen displays at society functions, and returned them eventually looking worth twice as much as they'd originally cost. In the interval between acceptance and return, they rested in the strongroom set in the wall at the far end of his office.

The firm had been established for two hundred years. Its strongroom was relatively modern, but Hammerstein was not up to date with his security. There was no time lock on the door; there were no invisible rays criss-crossing the area in front; there were no touch alarms, heat alarms, or pressure alarms beneath the carpet. There was simply the combination, and a wheel that turned back the lock. But it was a good combination, with no aural clicks, and no sense of touch to its tumblers.

4

The younger brother, Gunnar, was tall and handsome, and, in other surroundings, casually charming. His charm had always worked before, though not with such critically important information as a strongroom's combination. He had charmed the numbers from Helen Strange, and this time it had taken a full month. He now approached the door with confidence. The dial numbers were visible without the help of the torch. His brother did not watch, or if he did, it was casually, not noting the numbers used. He registered, perhaps, that it was a four-figure combination. But he was restless.

With a gesture almost theatrical Gunnar rotated the wheel. The locking pillars slid back with a sigh, and the door swung open.

The interior was six feet in height, with no more than a shoulder's width between the shelves. A man of Gunnar's breadth had to edge in sideways. The shelves were lined with metal trays, and the full depth of the strongroom was no more than four feet. The treasures left to Hammerstein's care did not occupy much space, and half the trays were empty. Gunner began to slide them out.

Niels, who had seen the light come on in the strongroom, was still pitched high with nervous tension, and ran to the slatted

5

blinds at the windows. Gunnar caught the movement in the corner of his eye.

'No.' Quite quietly.

Niels stopped, realising. The closed blinds would be a signal of their presence.

'Then move it.'

He drew out from beneath his sweater a calico bag and moved back towards the strongroom. Gunnar had a black velvet drawstring bag in his hand, and was holding it out.

\* \* \*

The man had not noticed the minivan, but his movement in the shadows attracted her attention. It was necessary to approach her quite closely to find the entrance her husband and his brother had used. She saw the shadow move into it. Without hesitation she reached forward, and drew the small automatic pistol from the shelf beneath the dashboard. She opened the van door quietly, stepped down onto the cobbles, then followed quietly. The window, left open, was noticeable at once. There was no sign of the shape she had followed. With the pistol tucked in the belt of her slacks, she jumped for the sill and drew herself up athletically.

★ ★ ★

As Gunnar handed the velvet bag to his brother, the intruder walked in on them. He was as large as Gunnar, in jeans and a denim jacket, but he'd prepared himself with a mask, amateurishly made from a balaclava helmet with a scarf stitched across mouth and nose. He was holding a pistol in his right hand, an automatic, which was not, at that time, detected as a reproduction. He said nothing. He held out his free hand.

He had timed it badly, and should have waited behind the door. The intention had been to wait until the calico bag, or whatever they'd be using, was full. This was only the first of the velvet bags. But there was no pressure, now. These two were clearly unarmed. He moved into the room, closer to the strongroom, and gestured with his gun. It was a good copy. He felt confident of the impression he made.

With no word spoken, the intention was clear. Gunnar should continue to hand out the velvet bags, and Niels to fill the calico one.

The woman walked in with the pistol in her hand. There was no doubt that this one was real. A lock of hair had escaped from her headscarf, but she in no way conveyed

7

an impression of dishevelment or panic. Her eyes were steady and cold.

The intruder realised that his position was now hopeless. He was in the centre of a triangle of opposition, with a toy gun, and with his left hand clasping the single velvet bag. There was a slight chance that he could get away with that one — that he might be allowed to. But he needed a diversion. With his shoulder behind it, he slammed the strongroom door.

Instantly she fired, a reaction from his movement. She had not aimed, but the shot took him in the left forearm. He dropped the velvet bag, stood for a moment, and then, in a gesture of almost childish pique, he threw his ridiculous toy at the strongroom door, and with something like a sob ran from the room.

Niels threw himself at the strongroom door. The wheel was solid. The lock had spun itself into locked position, and the combination dial had rotated automatically. He turned to her wildly.

She had not spoken. The hand at her side still held the pistol; the other hand had its knuckles pressed against her teeth. Niels knew what he had to do, and realised he could not attempt it with Gunnar's wife fluttering around him.

'Get out of here.'

She stared into his face. She knew he was unstable, liable to break down into fury under pressure. This was pressure, and his fury would stifle him. He needed, always, someone against whom he could direct it, and if she were here, then he might direct it at her. Alone he could, perhaps, control it. She turned away. There was, possibly, something she could do.

'Take it,' he snapped, his voice breaking.

He was pointing at the velvet bag on the floor. Angrily, annoyed that he'd think of such a thing at that time, she bent and swept it up. Then she was gone.

Left alone, he faced the strongroom door. Only Gunnar knew the combination, and he was inside. Niels was aware that he was close to breaking. He stood and drew in heavy breaths. Then he took up the crowbar, tapped on the door, and put his ear to it. Nothing. The door was blastproof, fireproof, and soundproof. He tried again, savagely this time, but he could detect no response from inside.

Then, aware that concentration and control were all that would help him, he stood before the door, and began.

One — one — one — one. Try it. No.

One — one — one — two. Try it. No.

And so on.

It was later calculated that he would have reached the correct combination in a little more than a week.

★ ★ ★

At eight-thirty the staff arrived. The police were at once informed. When the patrol car arrived, Niels was still working at it, snarling at anyone who came near. He was kneeling in front of the door by that time, his face distorted by tension, and sweat streaming from him.

Seventeen — three — nine — seven. Try it. No.

Seventeen — three — nine — eight. Try it. No.

Two policemen dragged him screaming to his feet. No one could understand what he was saying, as it was in a foreign language. After he had been sedated he was taken away, but by that time Helen Strange had arrived. She opened the door. Gunnar was dead, quietly in a slumped heap on the floor with one of the metal trays still in his hand. With a small cry, she collapsed beside him.

Two hours later Helen Strange was arrested. It was thought she could not have realised the theft would point directly to her, as one of the only two people knowing the combination. But three days later, when Niels Bergh was able to speak coherently, and this time in English, the truth became more clear. Gunnar, the younger brother, had had to work hard on this one, but behind Miss Strange's quiet and cool exterior there had lurked a warm and rapacious woman, who could be persuaded with promises of a wild escape to romantic foreign lands and a life of excitement. When Gunnar had contacted her in the jazz club, where her sublimated soul found some release, she had apparently seen him as some sort of talisman, and had seen visions of wide expanses of freedom.

But Gunnar had made a mistake. Once he had the combination, he had not revisited the club. And there was delay. Niels was nervous, and himself had to be persuaded. Four days went by, and Helen Strange became afraid, realising what she had done, and with her dreams shattered.

The rest was guesswork. She could not force herself to go to the police, even less to her employer, but she would have to turn to someone. Had she confided to a friend? It was likely. Had she hoped that an intervention by that friend would prevent the theft? That, too, was possible. She was not a person who read other people's minds with any clarity, and could not have known that opportunity sometimes has to be seized. If only with a toy pistol.

But Helen Strange, though perhaps not very bright, was at least loyal. She never revealed the identity of the masked intruder. That such a timid, quiet creature could hold out so successfully against expert interrogation surprised everyone. In court she spoke not a word. It was only later, when she was transferred from Holloway to a mental hospital, that the truth became apparent — her mind had collapsed.

After all, it was she who had opened the strongroom door.

Two weeks later, Gunnar's wife was arrested in Stockholm. She denied any knowledge of the jewels that had been in the black velvet bag, and was committed to Holloway for three years. Niels, her brother-in-law, got eight years.

It was a pity that the jewels had not great intrinsic value, as they were not in their settings. They consisted mainly of sapphires, with a few emeralds and rubies, and were from an eighteenth-century Finnish necklace. In their settings they became a Finnish national treasure, which could be valued only in terms of national pride, which, with the Finns, was immense. Out of them they were virtually worthless.

It was the metal tray containing the settings that Gunnar was found to be gripping in his right hand. Apparently, he had been tapping out the combination with it on the inside of the door.

# 1

My day had been a complete washout, but an hour from home the rain eased, and by the time I turned into my drive the stars were shining. The bungalow was dark and quiet. I told myself that this could mean she'd returned home and gone to bed. Complete self-deception. The despair had soaked into me and I knew it was a delusion. Besides, the garage door was open, and there was no sign of her red Mini.

The garage door was open — and I'd left it locked!

It was an effort to climb out of the Dolomite. I stood very still, not allowing the car door to slam. You never completely lose the instinct, and though I'd been six years out of the force, the same old prickling was there. I'd had intruders, and they could still be there.

I left my camera holdall on the back seat and stepped sideways onto the lawn. The weariness of the long drive seemed to drain out of me, and I was tense, moving forward on the balls of my feet, into the deeper shadows of the trees. With my head low I reached the front window and carefully, in the corner, raised my eyes above the sill.

Nothing. No flicker of light, or movement of the shadows. And yet . . . the shadows were not exactly where they should have been. There had been a displacement of the furniture.

Then, heart pounding, I knew what it could mean. I straightened. No hesitation now, because my original suspicion of intruders seemed to be unfounded. Karin had been home! And left again? That possibility was appalling to consider. That she'd been gone four days, leaving no word or message, was bad enough. It had driven the heart from me. That she could sneak back, possibly to collect some of her things, at a time when she'd know I was on a job in Yorkshire and would be away all day . . . that was mortifying.

I plunged for the front door and fumbled with the key, swung it open, and darted my hand to the light switch.

'Karin!'

The bungalow had the feel of emptiness, as though the air had settled and become sluggish. My voice was tiny and inadequate. I turned to close the door, and noticed for the first time that there was a hole in the glass beside the lock. My feet, when I moved them, tinkled in it.

The anger and shock at having to face a break-in, after all, was only slightly buffered by the thought that at least it hadn't been Karin who'd degraded me. For a moment my emotions clashed, and I couldn't move. So many times I'd struggled to understand the distress of burglary victims whom I'd interviewed, but I'd never quite absorbed from them the shock of personal assault. Now I knew. Every nerve cried out in outrage. They'd laid their filthy hands on my life.

They had, too, politely placed my mail and newspaper on the hallstand.

It was ridiculous that I didn't know what to do. Shock held me, and I do not remember walking into the front room until I was there with my finger on the switch, but with fear preventing me from putting it on. I was afraid to see what they had done, and already my stomach was heaving. Without conscious volition I depressed the switch.

Then the light from the chandelier fixed it in my mind, like the flash from my own camera outfit. A complete shot, in colour, gradation perfect, colours for some reason too bright, but accurate, with every detail superb.

They had wrecked the room. I drew in my breath. But still, behind it all, I felt strangely calm. I was simply observing. Karin's cut-glass collection had been swept onto the floor from their cabinet, the books tumbled, scatter-leaved, from the low bookshelf, my hi-fi torn out and dumped across the rug, the vases smashed against the wall, and the roses I'd replaced fresh, in case she returned, lying in the hearth. Amongst the flowers were the remnants of Karin's own yellow vase, which she'd made herself when she was fourteen. 'I used to go to my Aunt Sigrid's place, Owen,' she'd told me. 'She let me practise on her wheel.'

It was strange that she hadn't taken it with her, I thought vaguely. She hadn't taken many of her clothes, either.

Still I had not stirred. My hand was over the switch, and time was not moving. There was a thought struggling to get through, and I tried to focus on it, forcing my eyes to absorb the scene. Then I had it. This had not been a burglary, because as far as I could see nothing was missing. It was a search, a frantic one, but a complete one.

Then training and routine took over. I was, again, a police officer, in somebody else's house, calm and observant and completely impersonal. I left the switch on, and went systematically through the bungalow, leaving lights on in every room.

Across the hall to the main bedroom. It was the same there, destruction and disorder, but nothing missing. The mattress and the base were both slashed open, sheets and cover scattered, pillows slashed and flock everywhere. They'd taken out the drawers from the dressing table and dumped their contents on the carpet, and stripped out the wardrobe. But nothing had been taken.

In the other bedroom, which was really a storeroom, it was a similar picture. Disorder and ransacking, but no theft. The same in the kitchen, and the same in the back room, which was my office. They had completely scrambled my filing system and cleared out the cabinet, but there had been something desperately systematic about it. They had even been through my diaries, though that could've given them little more than a picture of my steadily growing professional stature as a photographer — more a picture of Karin than of me, because it was she who'd given me the self-confidence and drive to pursue it so intensely.

Eventually, stomach now in control and my outrage cooled, I went into the kitchen and filtered some coffee. The anger now was that it was something I couldn't understand, when I already had enough on my mind worrying about Karin. Four days, and not a word!

19

Could this be linked with her extraordinary behaviour? Could it, I wondered, possibly *no* be linked with it?

It had been a careful search. At first I'd thought it was for money, or some such valuables, but my petty-cash box had been gone through and the money in it untouched. The fact that the search had been unsuccessful was indicated by the very completeness of it, as there'd have been no sense in going on after any successful discovery. The fact that this was not a simple mindless loutishness for its own sake was proved by the failure to pour treacle and sauce over the carpets and urinate on the bed.

I drank coffee, and was no further forward when I'd finished it. It didn't do its work. I was exhausted, and could barely stay awake, and I didn't want to think about it any more. Shock numbed my mind. For four days it'd been pummelled for an explanation of Karin's desertion of me, and I could do without anything like this to worry about. I'd come to depend on her. She was the driving force of my life, and I was gradually running down without her.

Miserably, I went to see whether I could make something out of the bed, and found myself, instead, on my knees in the front room, gathering up the remnants of her vase.

How *could* she have left it?

There was no possibility of repairing it — the bits were too small. The only two pieces large enough to fit together — and they did not join when I tried them — were from the thicker base. I turned them over.

On one piece, in black under the glaze, was the abbreviated word: 'Sil — ', and on the other an ending: ' — mics'. And on the first piece, put in the wet clay with a toothpick or something, her initials. K.B. Karin Bergström. Fifteen years ago she'd done that. She'd weep when I told her. If I ever did. If I could come face to face with her, and ask her why the hell she'd done this to me. Four years to build it up, and four days to smash it, like the vase at my feet.

Then, beneath one of the roses, I saw the corner of a piece of white card, slipped it out, and turned it over. It was a colour photograph that I'd seen before, but only once, right at the beginning. She must have put it into the vase, which would explain why she'd never put flowers into it. She had kept two milestones of her life together.

She had been sixteen at the time — and the vase two years old. God, but she'd been beautiful even then, though now

21

she'd matured and was more serious. In the photograph she was all vivacity and eagerness for life, and was trying to control her laughter for the photographer, and her wonderful grey-green eyes were almost hidden. I knew every plane of that face, having taken dozens of shots of it, the proud line of her nose, the soft curve from jaw to chin, and every nuance and subtlety of her mouth. But in the picture it was all younger, all more delicate, though with the character already there.

She seemed to be standing in front of a church. I knew well the deep shadow of such an arched doorway behind her. She was wearing some sort of folk costume.

She had a red ribbon controlling the silken blonde of her hair, and was wearing a white, long-sleeved blouse with a heavily-flowered scarf draped over it. (Blossomed, I recalled, she had called it.) There was a red, embroidered corselet lifting her immature breasts (which weren't like that any more), laced across the front and apparently part of the skirt or apron. It was difficult to decide which. The apron was vertically striped in fine lines of white, red and black, and it almost obscured the flared black skirt beneath it. She was wearing (nearly out of the picture) flat-heeled soft black shoes, with red pom-poms on them.

Staring at it, kneeling there with my knees aching and my eyes moist, I was for a moment assaulted by a wave of despair. Then I forced myself to my feet, and went to the phone in the hall and reported the break-in to the police.

This was more from instinct than anything else, a throw-back to my few inglorious years in the force. A crime had to be reported. I was advised to get a bit of sleep, and a man would be round in the morning, sir. Not Owen, I noticed, not Mr Tanner, though he'd have known me. The same old sergeant, still duty officer at the desk. I couldn't remember his name. Worth a laugh, that, but I was way beyond laughter.

I finally slept, telling myself that the incident had to be connected with Karin, and that it in some way made her leaving less personal.

It proved nothing. I was as lost as ever. But I was asleep before that rationalisation came along to taunt me.

# 2

They sent me Richard Kent, or rather, he sent himself, as he was now a Detective Inspector, and could make his own decisions.

A shave and shower work wonders, and I'd had time to brew a pot of tea and singe a few slices of toast. I was alive and aware, and looking for some way of fighting back. You take it and take it, and then you have to lash out . . .

I opened the door to Dick Kent, who'd been my friend, as close to being a friend as anyone, and my left shoulder was low, my left foot advanced, chin down.

He said 'Take that look off your face, Owen. This isn't something you can bust by punching me in the face.'

I made a gesture, half apology, and stood back.

'Sorry, Dick. You're the only one around. I've got a pot of tea just made.'

He strolled in, swinging my camera holdall in one hand, my tripod in the other — the tripod Karin had bought me — six feet two inches, and brawnier than I remembered him, round face smiling and his eyes always friendly. Well, not always. I'd faced up to him once. One of my bad days when things had fallen apart and I'd been after his blood. My friend, Dick Kent, who'd reported me for failing to bring in . . . oh, what the hell! Why keep harking back? He brought in my equipment and said, 'You left your car door open, Owen. Getting careless, old son.'

I registered the fact that next door's ginger cat was hovering at his heels, but wary of him. It was a fine June morning and he was casual in slacks and a shirt open at the neck. I took the equipment from him.

'They've been through the car, too,' he said, to save me going to look.

He followed me into the kitchen. 'There's some toast if you want it,' I offered, but he shook his head. His eyes were everywhere, but that was no more than professional habit.

I looked through the holdall, but it was all there, my Canon A-1, the three lenses I'd taken, the flashgun, though I'd been a fool to think it'd be useful with steeplechasers when it rained. Nothing had gone, though there was a lot of money tied up in there. The tripod, too. Karin had said it was made of a special alloy tube, and it was very rigid, very light. Dick tossed the car keys onto the table. My front door key was on the same ring. He smiled into my startled eyes.

'You left 'em in the door.'

I groaned.

'Shaken you up, hasn't it?' he asked, taking a seat at the table. He admired the pattern on the Formica surface, giving me time to decide how to answer.

I sat opposite him, then got up to get him a cup and saucer. I poured, reached for the piece of toast that had one bite out of it, and looked up at him under my eyebrows.

'Don't you want to look around?'

He shrugged. 'Nothing missing, is there?'

'Not a thing.'

'Well then — '

'You're taking my word?'

'One thing you were always good at,' he commented casually. 'Always thorough, even with the truth.'

He didn't say what I hadn't been good at, which was sticking to a steady line and not plunging ahead on my own.

'No fingerprint men for me?' I asked. 'Don't I rate that?'

'Would you expect any prints?'

'No.'

He smiled, sipped his tea. We'd covered it all.

Dick had always been the placid, waiting type, not pounding away with questions, just letting it appear in its own time. The self-evident he never troubled himself with.

'Then why did you come?' I asked. 'I heard you'd made Inspector. What's a break-in to you?'

'Call it a friendly visit,' he told me kindly, as though genuinely attempting to calm my anxiety. 'We like to keep in touch with our ex-officers.'

'Oh . . . sure. But not too often.'

'We like to know you're making out. How long's it been now? Six years since you left us . . .'

Left. One way of putting it. I'd been allowed to resign. The alternative had been dismissal, which would have required them to give reasons. In writing. I'd dreaded that. Inadequate, and tries too hard to compensate! Ye Gods, the Chief Super had told me that to my face. The words had burned their way into my brain, though I'd provided my superiors with a more solid charge. Striking a senior officer.

'Six,' I agreed, but there was nothing in my voice to let him know I cared. 'And I'm doing fine. Just fine.'

'Married, I hear.' He was looking beyond my head to the window, and I could hear the cat scratching out some more of my putty. I glanced round.

'Next door's,' I told him. 'Not mine.'

'You haven't got a cat of your own, then?'

'No.' When in doubt, use one word at the most.

'Perhaps she didn't like cats.'

'Didn't?' I said sharply. He was smiling right through me, his soft brown eyes empty. 'You know something?'

'Only that she's left you.'

He knew too much. 'Which was why you used the past tense, I suppose?'

'Why else?'

It provoked a thought that had not crossed my mind. I'd been too absorbed in my own predicament, but not for one moment had I thought of her as anything but alive.

'What is it you know?' I jerked out.

'Only that she's left you.'

'You were suggesting she could be dead.'

'Was I? Owen, you jump down people's throats. Do *you* think that?'

'No.'

'Then we must hope not.'

I hadn't missed the 'we'. It was another of his smooth lead-ons. I was supposed now to demand why it should interest the police. To me it was a domestic matter, and he was suggesting that to him it was much more. I munched toast. It was suddenly too dry for my throat. But the swallowing gave me time to control my reactions.

'What *is* this, Dick?' I asked him, calmly enough. 'There's something I don't know. Why're you talking like this?'

'Shall we say we like to keep interested in our ex — '

'I *am* an ex-copper. Don't try to flannel me.'

'All right,' he conceded, having primed me sufficiently. 'Tell me about your wife. Karin, isn't it?'

'You know too much.'

'Tell me more. You've been married . . . how long?'

I grinned at him. 'I bet you've dug into the marriage records.'

He nodded. 'Birmingham Register Office. Four years and two months ago. In April. Karin Bergström. Swedish citizen.' He stopped, waiting.

'It rained,' I told him. 'She was wearing powder blue. It ruined her hair-do.'

'Bet she was mad.'

'Not a bit of it. Laughed about it. She takes the rough with the smooth.'

'She took you — '

'I was the rough part, yes. The smooth . . . damn it, that's none of your business. What the hell're you after, Dick? Tell me, and I'll try to help.'

He was peering into an empty pack of cigarettes. I'd never known him when he smoked his own. He looked across at me, like a lost, overgrown schoolboy — one of his acts. You always felt he had to be helped along. God, he was good. I threw him my pack.

'It's your last,' he told me, taking it.

'I'll dig out my pipe.' I wanted the excuse.

I did that. It involved going through into the front room and hunting through the mess to find my pipe and pouch. It also gave me time for a look out of the window. Dick had come in a red Allegro, and there was no sign of any back-up support.

It was my meerschaum. The tobacco was dry. I went back to him, and he was standing by the window, staring out at my meagre and overgrown garden.

'Could do with a bit of time spent out there.'

I laughed. Time? Karin had absorbed all my time, one way or the other. I sat. There was more tea in the pot, and he slid into the chair opposite me.

'A present from Karin,' I told him, filling the pipe. 'She told me I ought to stop smoking cigarettes.'

'Did she have to tell you what to do?' he asked.

'Advise.'

'You didn't take it, though.'

I looked a query at him over my cup.

'The tobacco's dry,' he pointed out.

'Pipes take a bit of getting used to. I'll have another go.'

'Symbolical.'

'What's that mean?'

'Her present.'

I scowled down at the pipe. He had a way of getting under my skin. All right, it was a comfort to handle it, because it kept me in contact with her. I was not keen on the depth of his perception. It showed he was trying hard, extracting every crumb from my crust of knowledge.

'And no letter left for you?' he asked at last, seeing that I wasn't going to take it up. 'No message? No hint?'

'I came home, and she simply wasn't here. Her car had gone, and some of her clothes.'

'She'd know where you were, that day?'

'She arranged my appointments. Yes.'

'So she'd know how much time she'd got. Time to pack the lot, perhaps. But she only took a few clothes, you say?'

And left her vase and the photograph. I saw what he meant. 'Yes. Left in a hurry.'

'Strange,' he commented. 'Don't you think

that's strange, Owen?'

I shook my head. He could take that as he liked.

The sun was shafting through the window onto my neck. It was nine-thirty, and I had an appointment in Birmingham. Dick seemed to be in no hurry. I decided not to ask him to leave, in case it gave him the idea he'd managed to unsettle me. The pipe was burning hot.

'Where did you meet her?' he asked.

'Oh . . . a club in Birmingham. I was on the prowl.' Caught his eye. 'Not that. Looking for photographic subjects. Somebody who'd model for me.'

He gave me a sceptical look. I ignored it. I'd been aiming high at that time, for the top. What I'd thought to be the top — fashion photography. Karin had attracted my attention. It was the way she'd held her head.

'And did she?'

I could now be lightly amused by the memory. Somehow, the idea had melted away. 'She posed. It's a different thing. But she'd got better ideas for me than fashion, and I hadn't got any clout with the fashion houses, anyway.' I smiled. 'Portraits, that's all she posed for.'

He seemed interested. 'Can I see one?'

No harm in that. I fetched him the framed one from the bedroom. The glass was cracked.

'Yes,' he said, and put it face down on the table. 'You think a lot of her, don't you?'

I felt myself flushing, with anger mostly. He was trespassing. I took the picture from him, and said nothing.

'It's in your voice,' he told me. He sounded sad about it.

'I've got work to do, you know,' I jerked at him.

He got to his feet, and I took him to the door. The cat was round there before we were.

'Keep us in touch,' he said. Then he drove away.

I went to check that he was correct about the Dolomite, and of course he was. It'd been searched. He hadn't mentioned the interesting fact that the house had been gone over while I was away, the car after I'd returned. Somebody was being very thorough indeed.

When I got back inside the cat was just finishing the remains of the toast. He'd always thought he lived with us, the people next door being a convenience he resorted to when we shoved him out.

I realised I wasn't thinking the same about

it now, and tried to analyse my emotions. It was straightforward enough. I was simply feeling less depressed. The police interest, the search of the house, the abruptness of Karin's departure, all these indicated she'd left on some emergency that I had to assume was valid. It did not necessarily connect with our relationship. She could well be just as upset about it as I was.

I went to the phone and rang Potter in Birmingham, to apologise for not turning up. It had meant a week's work at his factory, taking hundreds of shots of his manufacturing processes. The selected few would finish as framed twelve by tens in colour, as a wall decoration for his conference room, and in a brochure for advertisement purposes. Karin would have handled the publication and presentation side, which was a little beyond me.

Luck was on my side. Potter had a strike on his hands. Count on at least a fortnight, he told me, sighing, and I tried to sound put out, when I was damned pleased.

I began to tidy up the place. It was while I was doing this that I discovered the bungalow was under observation. That fact wasn't surprising, after Dick Kent's visit, the surprising thing was that the amateurish technique was not what I'd expect from the police. He was simply hanging around, walking back and forth, pausing opposite my drive. And never letting me get a glimpse of his face.

I thought of dashing out and demanding his business. I didn't get round to it.

This was late in the evening. All day I'd been tidying, with a couple of meals when I felt like it, so that the first two sightings of my watcher had not irritated me too much. The third — when he seemed to be a different man — annoyed me intensely. I was on my way to the front door, actually passing the phone, when it rang.

'Yes?' I snapped.

Karin's voice came through, clear and heart-catching.

'Is that you, Owen?'

'Karin! Where are you? Are you all right? I'll come — '

Her voice spoke through me, emotionless and repressed. 'I'm sorry, Owen . . . not meaning you to — '

I cut in desperately, aware that I had to fasten on every word. 'I missed that. Say it again.'

'I didn't mean you should be upset.'

'Upset? I'm nearly crazy.'

A pause.

'Karin — '

'Owen, it is nothing you could . . . so please do not question me.'

I was losing the odd word here and there, about every ten seconds.

'Could what?'

'Could understand. But please — '

'I'd understand if I can meet you. Where are you?'

She ignored that. 'Is the . . . still there?'

'Oh, for God's sake! Is the *what* still there?'

'The man,' she said, her voice fading as though she'd turned away from the phone. 'The man watching the house.'

The phone was slippy in my hand. I was hot and distraught. 'He's there. What about the man?'

'Did you say he's there?'

'Yes. What about him?'

'He's been watching for more than a week.'

I gasped at that. There wasn't anything I could think to say.

' . . . happened?' she asked.

'What? I've got to see you.'

'Has anything else happened?'

'My wife has left me. She just went away.'

'Say it again, Owen. I missed that.'

'Can't you hear me clearly?'

'Very clearly. Has there . . . else happened?'

Even with the missing word, I knew that question now.

'Somebody's broken in and searched the place.'

I heard her breath hiss between her teeth. For a moment I had a clear and distressing image of her big eyes grave and her lower lip tucked between her teeth.

' . . . take anything?'

'Didn't take a thing.' I was impatient. Why were we talking about this?

'Did you say break?'

'No, Karin. Take. Nothing taken. Stuff broken, yes. Your vase, Karin.'

'Ah!' Some other sound, but I lost it in another gap.

'The Mini,' I managed to remember. 'The brakes aren't good. Please stay where you are, and I'll come to you.'

'No, Owen.' There was another pause. Then she said: 'I cannot talk any more. The snow is blowing around my ankles, and I'm freezing — '

'Snow? This is June.'

'It's a . . . here.'

'A what?'

'Storm, Owen. *Do* listen.' That was her temper. I'd rarely heard it. She was under strain.

37

'I'll come to you,' I pressed in. 'Tell me where you are.'

There was silence.

'Karin! Karin!' I shouted.

Another silence. Then she spoke. 'You must not try to . . . me.'

'To find you? Of course I must try,' I protested.

I was losing her. Then, with her voice suddenly gasping, she cried out: 'No . . . no —'

The phone went dead. It had been a cry of pain. I shouted at it, but there was nothing. Nothing.

Then I ran out into the street, looking for something to thump, but the watcher had gone.

Shaking, I went back inside and sat in the kitchen, and wrote down every word of that telephone conversation, before I could forget it. I had to study it, and extract every inflexion of meaning in it. I worked out the timing. The word-gaps appeared to me to come at regular intervals of about ten seconds, but each one had been no more than a second in duration. From anywhere in Britain, with the caller feeding in coins, I'd have had gaps of around three seconds, but they'd have been wider spaced.

Must not try to find her? To hell with that!

I phoned Kent's office, but he'd gone home. I left a message that Karin had phoned, but I knew he'd sneer at it. Then I looked in the phone directory for the dialling code for Sweden, and called my friend Bertil Lindvall.

Bertil had a plastics factory in Västerås, and had opened a British branch in South Wales. I had done some work for him there, and we'd become firm friends, our mutual interest being photography — he was a stereo buff — and the fact that my wife was Swedish. 'Any time you're in Västmanland, drop in and see us,' he'd said. 'I'll show you what they look like on the screen.' Proud of his slides, he was.

He'd been good enough to give me his private phone number. I got him, and he'd obviously been halfway through his evening meal.

'Owen?' he asked, chewing.

'Owen Tanner.'

'My good friend!' his voice boomed. 'Where are you?'

'In England.'

'But the voice is so clear.'

'Do something for me, Bertil, will you?'

'But of course.' Then his voice rose to a

roar as he turned his head away. 'Margit, it is Owen.'

I felt warm, as I had in his presence. I asked him if he'd call their weather people to find out if it was snowing anywhere in Sweden. 'Go far enough north,' he said, 'and it is sure to be.'

'Not too far,' I said, hoping it wouldn't be.

'It's blowing a gale, here.'

'Find out where, Bertil. Will you do that?'

He would. The unquestioning acceptance of friendship.

'And then call me back,' I asked him. 'From a phone booth.'

'But I have my own phone — and it would take a pocketful of kroner.'

'No more than twelve, Bertil,' I told him, having counted the gaps.

Mystified but cheerful, he promised to do what I required, and he must have skipped the rest of his meal because he was back in ten minutes.

'A freak storm in Dalarna,' he told me. 'And that is not far north from here. Why the . . . Owen?' He sounded a little breathless.

'The what?'

'The phone booth. The wind is freezing my ankles.'

I explained why the phone booth. I'd

wanted to time the word gaps. Ten seconds. He said the phones in Sweden had coin slots at the top, and you simply perched a crown there, so that every time the previous one ran out the next one dropped automatically. It explained the very short gaps in the conversation. I thanked him sincerely.

'When shall we see you, Owen? You and dear Karin.'

I'd not mentioned Karin's involvement in this. 'Perhaps sooner than you think.'

'There it goes again. My last kroner. Did you say soon?'

'Perhaps, Bertil. And thanks again.'

In the morning I drove into town and went to a travel agency. They booked me a bunk in a four-berth cabin on the ferry, two days ahead, with accommodation for my car.

It gave me time to dig out my passport and stop the milk and papers and tell the cat I'd be away for a while, and time to decide which camera to take with one flashgun and the tripod, because I intended to travel as no more than a simple tourist.

And time to buy a map of Sweden.

Dalarna was a large county three hundred miles north-east from Gotenburg, which was where I'd land in Sweden. There didn't seem much to go on, but I'd got to do something or go crazy.

# 3

I was leaning over the rail when the *Tor Scandinavia* pulled away from the dock at Felixstowe. It was one-thirty, a fine afternoon, with a coolish north-easterly breeze. I was watching the transverse propellers easing the nose out. A Greek cargo ship was loading, and somebody waved. As my elbows were resting on the rail, and my Canon in my hands, I got a shot of him. For a moment there was the illusion that I was really a holidaymaker, enjoying the moment. But surprisingly few people were doing the same thing, and only about a dozen were up there with me.

As we drifted out into the channel the breeze was considerably stronger, and I became aware that I was alone, and cold. I walked back to the nearest hatch door, and into the warmth of Deck 6.

The crossing would take twenty-three hours. It seemed an eternity. I started to walk down to the second deck, where my cabin would be.

Down there, in amongst the engines, it seemed that the sea swell was accentuated.

I was in a maze of narrow corridors, and following a profusion of helpful direction signs. The cabins were each long enough to sleep in, and wide enough to stand between the bunks, two each side. I found my cabin. One person was in an upper bunk. A man. Well, it would be, wouldn't it? I wondered whether I'd have drawn a woman if my name had been Hillary.

He swung his legs down. He was in sweat shirt and jeans, a tall, good-looking young blond, with no hair on his chest.

'We the only ones in here?' I asked.

'Ja,' he said, bringing it out something like Yorr. 'That is how it is, I think.' He leaned forward and stuck out a huge, bronzed fist. 'Anders Norgren,' he said.

'Owen Tanner.' I winced. 'You Swedish?'

He threw back his head and laughed. 'You are good guessing.'

He allowed me to revive what was left of my hand. 'Just tracing the cabin,' I told him. A claustrophobic would have gone mad in ten minutes. He was quite relaxed. 'I'm sorry if I disturbed you.'

He grinned. 'It is nothing. I was resting. I have travel all night and day. In Scotland, fishing the salmon, and a cablegram from my employers — I am needed at home.'

'It's very satisfying to be wanted.' I

wondered why he hadn't taken the ferry from Newcastle. 'I'll see you again.'

I left him to catch up on his sleep and began the long climb up through the decks. There was a lift, but you need to know which deck you want, and I didn't.

I found the cafeteria somewhere around the fourth deck. It was open and there was a queue. I'd driven 180 miles without a break, so I was hungry, but I can't stand queues so I went and sat at one of the tables by the row of windows, where the spray was already beginning to obscure the glass, and waited. I lit my pipe, decided to visit the duty-free shop for some more tobacco, and allowed my eyes to go out of focus. Once more, for perhaps the hundredth time, I tried to make sense out of what I already knew.

If Karin had simply intended to leave me flat, why had she phoned? That thought I clung to, but I had to remember that she had not been encouraging. There'd also been an impression that she'd not been alone in the phone booth. Her last cry: 'No . . . no — ' need not have been intended for me. 'No . . . no . . . you must not try to find me,' that could have been meant for me. But, 'No . . . no . . . I want to say more,' could have been directed to someone forcing the phone from her fingers. All I'd got had been,

'No . . . no — ' and the distress in her voice. I'd got that clear enough.

The ship lurched with a thump, and spray clittered on the glass. Yet the sea seemed calm, with only a shallow swell. I looked round. The queue was shorter.

Memories were crowding my mind, now that I was reaching for them eagerly. Her voice! Of Karin, her voice was the easiest to remember. She spoke a lilting, almost-perfect English. She could be serious and skittish in alternate moments, and was always driving me on with a critical understanding that surprised me, encouraging me, scorning my lack of confidence, cooling my flights of romantic endeavour. But I had to try desperately to concentrate my memory on less emotional matters, to be practical and recall whatever might help me.

I thought she had mentioned having lived in Stockholm, but there'd been holidays on a lake. Everybody in Sweden took holidays on lakes — they've got thousands of them. 'The lake where I was born, Owen. On a clear day you could see the dome of the church across the water from our chalet.'

It didn't help. None of my fleeting memories helped. The queue was getting smaller. I levered myself to my feet.

A man was walking along the deck outside,

one hand to the rail, the breeze pressing his nylon mac against his legs. His head was bent, but I knew that line of the shoulders. It was Kent.

I was moving in a second, and lurched forward to intercept him. At once I became aware that the ship was rolling more than I'd realised. I stumbled, pitching from one chair back to the other. I was aiming for the nearest door, shot out into the ship-width walkway, and groped for the handle of the hatch.

The wind flung me out, the door nearly tearing from my hand. I turned, forcing it back into its frame, then staggered over to the rail. Spray was whipping from the bow, and the green steel deck was empty of everything but a moving sheet of water.

His attention must have been attracted by my abrupt movement, and he'd disappeared in the other direction. I cursed as a sheet of spray was thrown up and descended on me. The salt was strong on my lips when I fought my way back inside.

I was wet and bedraggled, my hair in a tangle over my eyes. There was a dark patch on the front of my jacket and my slacks were clammy against my knees. The bulk of my luggage was locked away in the car, so I hadn't got a change with me. It meant finding the nearest gents and cleaning up with handfuls of their disposable tissue. Then I returned to the cafeteria.

The queue had gone. I collected a beefburger and chips, with a side salad, and took it with a bottle of lager to a table by the port windows, where the spray was less, keeping an eye on the deck outside. Because of this the voice at my shoulder startled me.

'Do you mind if I join you?'

I glanced up. It was Dick Kent, immaculate in slim, fawn slacks and a maroon Norfolk jacket. His shirt was open at the neck, with a silk Paisley scarf knotted tastefully to hide his too-prominent Adam's apple. There was no sign of moisture on him, no surprise in his brown eyes.

'I spotted you,' he said, 'but you ran away.'

I grunted. He, at least, had facilities for a complete change. He had a piled plate involving smoked salmon and shredded carrots. He put it down carefully and smiled with warmth.

'There's really no point in carrying this pretence to such lengths,' he said.

'Pretence?'

'That you don't know where to locate your wife.'

I clattered the fork onto the plate angrily.

47

'Now look here . . . ' Then I eyed him suspiciously. 'Is that why you're following me?'

'My dear Owen!' His most expansive manner. 'You bristle all over. I am not following you. This is my holiday.'

'Brought your car?' I asked.

'Well . . . no. I never do. This is a regular trip for me. Across to Göteborg,' he declared, waving a fork and using the Swedish pronunciation with smug familiarity, 'then another boat through the canals and lakes, finishing up at Stockholm. A week there — '

'I left you a message.'

'Oh . . . that.'

'I told you that Karin phoned.'

'I expected it.'

'That she'd phone?'

'Rather, that you'd claim she had.'

He was devious, always had been, but now he found a delight in it. 'Otherwise,' he added, 'you wouldn't have had an excuse to head for Sweden yourself.'

He was getting on my nerves. 'What's the point in this? You'd surely tapped my phone.'

Then he frowned, a mere flicker of expression behind his eyes. He hadn't applied to have it tapped.

'But,' I said softly, 'there was no mention of Sweden.'

He was not going to believe that. He lowered his eyes to his plate and took a gulp of lager. The dining area was now half empty, and somebody was clearing the tables.

'Well . . . ' He swallowed. 'I hope your visit is successful. I haven't met your wife.'

And wouldn't, if I could help it. He was far too smooth.

'Though of course . . . ' he chewed placidly, 'I might never have the chance.' Looked up into my eyes. 'Not alive, anyway.'

My hand was quivering, with the knife gripped rigidly in it. That was the second time he'd suggested Karin could be dead.

'I spoke to her on the phone.' I wasn't sure he could hear me. Mainly I'd said it to myself, softly, for reassurance.

'So you said.'

'Damn you, why didn't you tap the blasted phone?' I demanded, banging the knife down on the table.

'Because you're so honest, Owen. I can believe you.'

'Then why're you calling me a liar?'

'Was I?' He said it in the same even tone, but there was something more imperative in his pause. I looked up to meet his eyes. 'Tell me in what way.'

I cleared my throat. Took up the knife again. Casually and easily, I told myself. This is no more than a game of words. 'You suggested she's dead, when I'd just told you I spoke to her on the phone.'

He was shaking his head, sorrowful at my lack of understanding. 'But you're heading for Sweden, and you also said she hadn't mentioned Sweden. There's a little lie, there, Owen. Not big. A little one.'

I met him head on, as calm as he was. I even smiled, having recognised his gambit. 'If you think I'm going to tell you *why* I decided to head for Sweden, then you'll have to try harder, Dick. I'm on holiday, too.' I patted the holdall on the seat beside me. 'A photographer's holiday.'

'And you wonder why I don't expect to see her alive!'

'What? What does *that* mean?'

'Mysteries, Owen. All over the place. A sudden disappearance, a house searched, a husband who gets mysterious phone calls and sets off on an unplanned holiday . . . d'you wonder why I'm worried? I think perhaps I get a whiff of danger to somebody. To her, d'you think? To you?'

I got to my feet, grabbed up my holdall. 'I've had enough of this. Keep your slick ideas to yourself.'

'Oh, come on . . . ' he said, 'sit down and stop flying off in all directions. Just tell me where you arranged to meet her.'

I turned and walked away from him. Too many of his insinuations were thrusting in on me. My life had been in chaos when he'd come to see me, and he'd succeeded in making things worse. I had to think, think . . .

My legs felt stiff, and I was completely unable to counter the movement of the deck. Bumping and crowding blindly, I headed for the fresh, salt air, pressed out into the wet wind, and fumbled towards the bow. This was the port side, with the spray less boisterous. I hung there on the rail, my mind groping for logic.

All I wanted was to find Karin, to meet her face to face, and ask her what it was all about. No more than that. Well . . . much more than that really. I wanted her, with words and gestures of encouragement, to persuade me that she would be coming home to me, soon, soon, and we could take up again . . .

But now Dick Kent had to haunt me with suggestions of a criminal background, even a dangerous one. Why couldn't they leave me alone?

Angrily, I turned from the rail. The woman

who'd moved up behind me — and who possibly had intended to speak to me — turned away at the same moment. I caught only a glimpse of the line of her jaw, beyond the edge of her fluttering red headscarf. But I knew that line. The turn of the head, the confident stride as she moved away . . .

I overtook her in three paces. The breeze flung back my lapel as I reached for her arm and caught her.

'Karin!'

She turned. Dark hair where Karin's had been blond, dark eyes to Karin's green-grey. But the line of the jaw . . . it changed as she opened her mouth, startled, then glanced down quickly to my fingers.

I mumbled something and thrust past her. She called out a few words, but I ignored them, pressing on quickly now with the breeze behind me, getting a wind-torn hatch door slammed between us. I couldn't have said why I ran from her.

I had stumbled into the bar, not recalling how I reached there. Soft music was playing, and it was nearly empty. I took a brandy into a secluded corner, and fought against any thoughts of Karin that were not pleasant.

Then the voice that had called me was clear and close. 'I'm sorry. I startled you.'

I forced myself to look up. With the headscarf thrown back and her hair loose, the style as well as the colour of her hair was completely different from Karin's. And it was foolish to have thought her jawline was similar. This young woman's was softer, fuller. Her eyes were farther apart and larger. But she was just as beautiful, in a darkly enigmatic way.

I'd spent so much time taking all that in that I saw the doubt, and then the embarrassment, clouding her eyes.

'I'm intruding,' she ventured.

I was on my feet. 'No . . . no, please.'

She smiled. Sunlight chased the shadows. 'I'll go away.'

Suddenly I needed her. She was something real, a contrast to Karin and to the confusion surrounding Karin. And she was there.

'Please stay.'

She seemed to understand my necessity. Without another word she drew back the chair opposite me, sliding a hand beneath her slacks, as though she more usually wore a skirt.

'I'll get you a drink,' I offered. Insisted.

She lifted one finger from the table surface. 'He's bringing it.'

And so he was, one of the men from behind the bar. I sat. She saw my surprise.

'They know me,' she explained, and it was not an explanation, smiling again in a way that soothed and calmed. The drink was clear and sparkling. We sat and stared at each other. Then I remembered my manners.

'I was very rude.'

'Oh no,' she protested.

'But I was. My name is Owen Tanner.'

'And I am Eija Karlsson.' It sounded like Aiya.

She stood. I followed suit. We shook hands gravely, in the Scandinavian manner. Then, seated again, she cradled her glass in both hands, and sipped her drink without taking her big, glowing eyes from me, and asked:

'You are going to Sweden on holiday?'

I was cautious. One hint of interest, and I have a tendency to say too much. 'Sort of.' Yet her interest was genuine.

She laughed gently. 'What kind of answer is that?'

'It describes it accurately.' Amused at my evasion, she was shaking her head. 'And you?' I challenged, still not relaxed.

She shrugged. Her eyebrows shrugged. They were unplucked. 'I am returning from a month's course at Cambridge. I have been polishing my English accent.'

Polishing? It sounded like BBC Grade 1 to me. I was interested. 'Oh?' I said.

'I do one month a year on one of them.'

'Them?'

'My languages.' She was being casual, but her modest pride shone through. She might have been twenty-five. For a moment she was in her teens.

'How many are there, then?'

'Six,' she said. 'And my own.'

'And what would that be?'

She sat back, her head cocked sideways, and then she came out with a sentence like a cascade of rocks down a Welsh mountainside. She smiled, and her face lit up. 'That is my own. It was Finnish for: 'You're trying to change the subject, Owen Tanner'.'

I hadn't recognised my name in that lot. 'Am I?' I couldn't recall it. 'What was that?'

'You and your holiday, which you described as sort of.'

I laughed. 'Call it a quest, then.'

'That,' she decided, frowning, 'is a word I do not know. Quest?'

'I'm searching for my wife, who has left me.'

'A Swedish wife?'

'Yes.'

'Is she very beautiful?' she demanded, as though that could be a distinct disadvantage.

'Very. Shall we go out on deck again?'

She looked at me severely. 'You don't want to go out there.'

And I knew I didn't. 'I do,' I protested. I hadn't wanted to discuss Karin.

'It is more quiet in here, and you were not happy out there. That I could see.'

She was quietly taking control. I should have turned and run again.

'I'll get you another drink,' I suggested.

'If you wish.'

I was on my feet. 'Gin and tonic, isn't it?'

'Lemonade,' she said severely.

'Do they serve non-alcoholic drinks?'

'I told you. They know me.'

I brought the drinks, and I was back to lager. I'd had a thought. 'You said where you'd been,' I reminded her. 'But not where you're going.'

'It doesn't matter.'

'You're stalling,' I said severely. 'And that's English for: 'You're evading the question'.'

Her eyes were big and dark. Her chin was quite sharp, her cheeks full and high. The lips quivered with controlled humour. 'Back to work, of course. I'm a courier.'

'For a travel firm?'

'For a shipping line that operates in the Baltic. I travel the pleasure cruises. I'll pick up my ship at Stockholm.' Then she sipped, raised her chin, and went on: '*Is* she very pretty? Do you have a picture of her?'

Of course I had. I produced the one of Karin in her gay costume. She studied it, pouting. 'She is very Swedish.' She turned it over, turned it back. 'That is her traditional folk dress. She is very young, here.'

'She was sixteen.'

'And now?'

'Twenty-nine.' To my thirty-five.

'And she's left you?'

'Yes.'

She considered it again, gravely. 'She doesn't *look* stupid. But people change.'

So I had to justify Karin. I told Eija Karlsson about my wife's encouragement, and the light she'd brought into my life. Eija was good at listening, and I was in this thing on my own. I needed a listener. Sometimes ideas solidify when they're expressed. Eija cocked her head, not commenting. I told her about Karin's desperate sense of order and neatness, and Eija nodded her pursed-lipped approval, so I searched my mind for other aspects that would attract the approval, because her lips, when pursed, were red and moist and worth watching. Then I told her how Karin had left me so abruptly, just so that I could watch her bated interest, her startled eyes. I told her, then, about the phone call, waiting, hoping for some comment about the snow in June.

'It can snow in Finland at almost any time,' she observed.

'And you?' I asked.

She said she didn't understand, but suddenly it mattered to me. She had said very little about herself, yet she had drawn so much from me, just with her intense interest and sympathy. I had to know that it was genuine, and not an amusing way of passing a dull half-hour. When she smiled she was curiously shy.

'You don't want to hear about me.' Knowing that I did.

And she at once plunged into a jumbled, almost incoherent account of her life and hopes and fears, her joys and excitements, of her father, who was a retired Chief of Police, now head of security at the Museum of Art Treasures in Helsinki, of her ex-fiancé, the pig, who'd gone off with a Greek pop singer.

'He must be stupid — no loss,' I supplied. We were even.

She spared me a mischievous smile, and plunged on. I was lost in the whirl of her exciting existence, fascinated, as I'd always been, by anybody who could speak seven languages — 'The first three are the most difficult' — who was something of an expert on Sèvres porcelain, could swim a respectable thousand metres, and belt a ball with some success round a tennis court. The tension flowed from me.

She glanced at her watch. 'It has been so pleasant talking to you,' she said. 'I must go. I'll wish you luck.'

I stood. 'In what way?'

'This quest of yours.' Her new word. She savoured it.

'Thank you.'

'Though I think you are very foolish.'

Then she walked away, her head high, taking her warmth from me and drifting out of my life. She nodded to the barman, and he grinned.

There were fourteen hundred people on that ship, and I was suddenly desperately alone. I would even have welcomed a word with Dick Kent, but I couldn't locate him. I went down to my cabin, to find that Anders Norgren had gone. I sat on the edge of a bunk dispiritedly, then abruptly I was very tired, lay back for a minute, and was almost at once asleep.

★ ★ ★

Down there, with only a glow of light in the cabin, time meant nothing. I awoke, put on my personal light, and saw that it was nearly ten. I assumed that had to be ten at night. I was hungry, but otherwise felt fine.

For a couple of minutes I tried to pack the holdall into one of the small lockers supplied, but couldn't manage it, so, after I'd freshened up and changed my shirt, I took it up with me to find something to eat.

There was still sluggish movement in the cafeteria, and I managed to get a ham roll and coffee. From somewhere there was music, the bass a heavy thud. I had a second coffee, and sought it out.

The bar was now crowded. A small combo, over-amplified, was playing pop with vigour, and a tall, slim man with bristles for hair stood at a floor mike in a white suit and a black tie and tried to sing. The bass was too heavy for the complex accoustics, and the man turned out to be a Swedish comedian, so I decided to try the open air.

The scene had changed. There was no swell, the sea so calm that the glow in the sky was barely ruffled as it melted into the water. I lit my pipe and absorbed the peace. No spray, now, no cool wind, just a gentle, mild breeze from the ship's passage. Softly, I could hear jazz.

At the stern there was a sun deck, played on now by the moon and the sky-glow. Leaning against the aft rail there were a pair of bearded young men in felt hats and jeans and baggy jackets, one playing bass chords on a guitar, the other a liquid flow of New Orleans jazz on a clarinet. A dozen people were standing around, listening. The clarinetist was good. They seemed to have their total possessions spread around them, and in another setting would have been buskers. But this was not for money, it was for the sheer joy of the moment.

They stopped. There was a patter of applause. The clarinetist bowed, not smiling, his face gaunt and humourless. His friend, bigger and bulkier, grinned with pleasure. Then they began again, a slow, langorous blues, and I looked about me.

Leaning over the far rail, looking away from me, were Eija Karlsson and Anders Norgren.

He had changed his clothes. I saw a heavily-checked sports jacket and grey slacks. He and Eija were laughing together. She now wore a skirt, I thought blue, but it looked black in that light, but she still wore the white, puff-sleeved shirt, with a red scarf at the neck, its points at the back.

My instinct was to walk away, but I moved

towards them. The blues sobbed. 'St James Infirmary', I realised. The chords were minor. They turned, sensing my approach, and Anders smiled.

'*Hej*,' he said.

'*Trevligt att se dig igen*,' said Eija.

'I'm glad to see you two have met,' I told them insincerely. But you have to be polite.

They made what the society papers describe as a splendid couple. Standing up, Anders Norgren was four inches taller than Eija, and the teasing of salmon in Scotland had given him a nice tan. He was too damned good-looking to be real. The knot of the scarf was at Eija's throat, her neck rising above it in a smooth, heart-catching line. They were from another world, walking on a breath of heaven in their own perfection. It seemed only natural that they'd have drifted together.

'What did you say to me?' I asked.

Eija laughed. 'That we are pleased to see you again.'

Anders beamed at me. 'Am I to be meeting you at the bar?' he asked.

'It's noisy in there.'

Eija nodded. 'But pleasant here.'

He inclined his head. 'I think I will be trying their lager,' he decided. He smiled at

Eija, for some reason shook my hand again, and drifted away.

'He plays tennis,' said Eija, watching his lithe, athletic frame melting into the shadows.

'He'd grip a raquet well. And speaks how many languages?'

'Only three.' But there was amusement in her voice.

'They're the most difficult.'

She took my arm. The clarinet sobbed into silence on a sour note, and I turned. An officer was speaking quietly to the two buskers. Their music was apparently superfluous to requirements. The gaunt one opened a black wooden box and stripped down the clarinet, bedding it in the prepared recesses. He had a brass-coloured sax in there, too.

'Let's find somewhere to kip down, Cowboy,' he said.

I touched his arm. The jacket was green corduroy, very old, tailored for wider shoulders. 'It was good.' Apologising for the officer.

He smiled. His cheeks were hollow, his eyes sunken.

'They're heathens,' he said.

When they'd disappeared into the shadows, Eija and I were virtually alone. There seemed nothing to say, nothing that needed saying.

We watched the light, which was taking an eternity to die.

'I'm down in the bowels of this thing,' I told her, meaning that I was in no hurry to get down there.

She did not reply. I saw that she had her face lifted, as though to the sun, her eyes closed. Her cheeks were peach in the dim, remaining glow.

'How will you get to Stockholm?' I asked gently.

Her eyes opened, and swivelled to me. 'By train from Göteborg.'

'You like trains?' It was over 300 miles to Stockholm.

She lifted her shoulders. 'It is wearisome. I like the clean air, but I didn't bring my car.'

'I have mine with me.'

She thought about that.

'You spoke about Dalarna,' she said quietly, at last.

'Only because it snowed there. But she once lived in Stockholm.'

I wasn't sure how much this was due to the perfection of Anders Norgren and his presence at her side. I was in no mood to rationalise, only to persuade myself that Karin could be anywhere in Sweden. It was only with Eija that I could find any peace.

'She could well be in Stockholm now,' I said.

'Yes.' Her smile was gently mocking. 'There is quite a lot of Stockholm, you know.'

'Quite a lot of Dalarna, too.' I nodded, urging her. 'There's a seat doing nothing in the front of the Dolomite. Are you in a great hurry?'

'In Stockholm, I would have spent three days alone in the flat I share with my friend.'

I smiled. It seemed obvious. 'Well, then — '

'I will,' she decided, 'think about it. But . . . ' And she put up a finger to admonish me. 'But you spoke so earnestly of heading for Dalarna. I would not want to divert you . . . no, not one single kilometre. She is very important to you.'

'She is,' I had to agree. 'And you will not.'

'Though you have not made me understand why,' she decided seriously. 'Do you always carry a camera?'

'What? Oh, it's part of me. If the light was good, I'd like to take you against this rail . . . ' My flashgun and tripod were in the car.

'How can you dance with that bag hanging

from your shoulder?'

'Dance?' I hadn't danced in years. I grinned at her. 'The same way you do, with that shoulder bag of yours.'

'I leave it on the seat. Let us go and find Anders.'

'Good idea. He can guard my camera, while we dance.'

She laughed, delighted at the thought. Her eyes flashed at me, sharing it.

So we danced. Anders had found himself a pert blonde who laughed too much, so I left the camera on my seat, and danced with abandon, Eija lithe and expert in my arms. For over an hour there was no worry about Karin, and all I had to do was find her. Suddenly it was all so simple.

We parted in the narrow passage beside the ganged fruit machines. I think I was a little drunk, Eija cold sober. An old lady was still working one of them. It was Eija's deck, and two o'clock.

'I have a double-berth cabin,' said Eija. 'To myself.'

It was a comment, by no means an invitation. She touched my arm, and was gone.

I lay awake in my bunk. Dalarna had to be the first objective. I told myself that, over and over, until I fell asleep.

Sometime in the night Anders Norgren slipped into the cabin, and retired to his bunk without putting on a light. The engines were a noticeable throb. A voice down the corridor asked for God's sake where was the lavatory. Otherwise, all was quiet.

I slept.

★ ★ ★

In the morning I managed to get a map of Sweden at the information kiosk, my other one being in the car. I took it in to breakfast. Eija wasn't anywhere I could see, but there was a restaurant, and they knew her, probably, there as well. The two buskers were sitting at a table in the corner. The thinner, darker one raised his eyebrows at me, so I took my tray over to them.

'You two eaten already?'

The big one called Cowboy was clutching his guitar, now in its plastic cover. 'Had coffee,' he said. 'Gotta watch the pennies.'

Were they that low? 'I'll treat you to cornflakes,' I offered.

His friend looked gloomy. 'Come on . . . man.' He was declining, but awkwardly, with a brash pride.

'And bacon and egg and sausages,' I tempted.

The pride had its limits. 'Well, now you're talking.'

'I dunno,' said Cowboy, embarrassed.

'Don't be a fool,' I told him.

So they ate with me. They'd washed, but shaving, like hair-cutting, was not part of their lifestyle. They told me they aimed to busk their way north into Lapland, then round into Finland, and eventually to Helsinki.

'Gotta see Helsinki,' said the gaunt one, whose name was Laurie.

I wondered what Helsinki had got to offer that was so entrancing.

'But we're thinkin' of going to Stockholm first,' Cowboy said, his mouth full of sausage. 'Can work up a stake there, we hear.'

'Not partic'lar, though,' Laurie qualified.

I nodded, looking round. No sign of her. I lit my pipe, and Laurie flapped his hand. 'Sorry,' I said. 'Man,' I added, and put it aside. I spread the map on my side of the table.

From Göteborg to Stockholm was almost due east, but very slightly north. For Dalarna, I could either head north, leaving the large lake of Vänern to my right, then keep going north-east, or I could head east along the E3 towards Stockholm, keeping Lake Vänern on my left, to the north of me, round the southern end of Lake Vättern, and *then*

68

decide to head north. The distance would be about the same, either way. The lads were interested.

All this I explained to Eija when I found her, which was some time later. I'd scoured the ship twice before I discovered her in one of the easy chairs by the twin cinemas.

'You are very persuasive,' she said, when I'd explained what I had in mind, a compromise, to ease her conscience.

'It would cover at least half of your route to Stockholm.'

'I would be . . . ' She sought the word. 'Imposing.'

'No. You speak Swedish. It would help.'

'You will find you do not need it in Sweden.'

'I know exactly what I need.'

She smiled, but it was hesitant, distant. 'Then I'll say thank you, and yes. But not for the reason you believe.' The thought seemed to worry her.

We were due to dock at one o'clock, Swedish time. We were together until the last moment, leaning over the rail to watch the craggy coast looming out of the lowering skies. The wind was brisk again, with wetness in it that carried no salt. The *Tor Scandinavia* edged between upthrusts of rock.

'It is going to turn cold,' she decided, sniffing the air.

'You can tell?'

'Yes. And I think it will rain.'

Then the call came for car owners to go to their vehicles.

'I'll see you the other side of Customs,' I said.

'It is better that I come with you in the car,' she decided, her eyes on the bronzed figure ten feet from us. Anders Norgren turned and smiled.

'*Det var trevlight att få träffa Er*,' he said.

'*Tack*,' she replied.

'What was that?' I asked as we moved away.

'He said it was nice meeting us.'

'Or you.'

'I thanked him.' She glanced at me. 'For both of us.'

With her two suitcases in the boot with mine, we drove together down the ramp onto Swedish soil.

# 4

The first spats of rain hit the windscreen as we drove away from the terminal. We turned between a vast complex of warehouses and cranes, my Dolomite hugging the right-hand lane. In front of me a G8 plate wandered over to the left.

'Look for E3 signs,' I said.

'I know. It's you who must look. You are the one driving.'

I glanced at her. She seemed remote — a young woman of moods. And nervous. Was she concerned about my driving ability on the wrong side of the road?

She noticed my movement. 'You are too generous, Owen.'

As I didn't know what she meant, I concentrated on the road. We seemed to be driving a long way to reach the main stream of traffic.

Way ahead of us, two figures were trudging, one behind the other and well in, extended thumbs working without optimism, with only the occasional glance over their shoulders. A felt hat with its brim turned down, a bush hat with its brim turned up, bobbles dangling from it.

'It's our friends.'

She peered. '*Your* friends.'

'Laurie and Cowboy.'

The rain pattered on the roof.

'They'll get soaked,' I said. 'Let's give 'em a lift.'

She said nothing.

'Well . . . why not?' I asked.

'It's your car.'

Then they seemed to spot me, and turned. Two thumbs, now with more hope and urgency. A friend!

I eased the throttle and coasted the last hundred yards, with all the correct signals because British drivers were crowding me nervously. I drew up beside them and winched down the window.

'Want a lift?'

Laurie stared at me without interest, only his deep-set eyes glowing. Cowboy grinned hesitantly. They had spotted Eija beside me.

'Don't wanna put you out,' Laurie grumbled, looking away and shuffling his feet. He was a gaunt tangle of bone and muscle, hard as his music was soft, and he was strangely tense.

But Cowboy burst out, 'Where you heading?'

Feeling Eija reproving at my elbow, I

threw the challenge at her. 'What about Stockholm?' I asked the lads.

At which, the rain now bouncing from their hat brims, they nearly tore off the doors getting in.

The Dolomite wasn't all that big, and the boot was full. They crowded the back seat, Laurie's black box on his knees, the duffle bag on the back shelf, nearly obstructing my rear vision, and the guitar moving tentatively in the general area of my left ear. I lifted my foot from the brake, and the automatic gearbox took up the drive. I spotted the E3 sign ahead.

'I've got to warn everybody,' I shouted, 'that I'm a lousy driver.' For some reason I was suddenly elated. Maybe burning a few boats now and then at least lights up the sky.

We were into the outskirts of Göteborg, swept into the stream of flyovers and multi-lanes. I had to concentrate, and make decisions well ahead. Nobody was saying anything, and the traffic flow was steady at fifty. I could feel Eija's tense disapproval. I at last leaned towards her.

'What chance would they have stood in this traffic?'

'It's not the point, and you know it, Owen.'

All I knew was that I wanted to keep her with me as long as possible, and Stockholm was as good a place as any to start looking for Karin. After all, it might well have been snowing in Dalarna, but that was three days before.

'I could have taken the train,' she murmured, 'and left you free . . . ' Her words petered out.

'Free to do what?' I demanded. 'To head north looking for Karin, when you clearly disapprove?'

She became silent. In the back, Cowboy was tuning his guitar. We were out into open country, with rock outcrops each side of the motorway, and the trees were beginning to close in.

You can see too many trees. The view was mainly of pines and silver birch, either looming on each side or parading into distant clouded hills. From time to time there was a brief glimpse of water, but it looked uninviting. The rain hammered down, and in the back Cowboy toyed with chords, and Laurie began to sing in a strange, nasal whine. The screen was beginning to steam, and I had to give it a touch of the heater. And in a week it would be midsummer!

Eija was silent.

Volvos and Saabs were overtaking me

steadily. I kept an eye open to the rear, there being only two lanes, and eased my right-hand wheels onto the reservation to let them through. In the end she told me about it.

'You should not do that.'

'Giving them room.'

'It is not necessary. Why do you have to be so polite, Owen?'

'I'll try not to be.'

But she was constrained by the presence of the two in the back.

We stopped for a break around four at a petrol station that boasted a café. There was a brief interlude in the rain. Eija and I took omelettes into a far corner, but the other two remained outside with a hamburger each. I supposed their funds wouldn't stretch too far.

Eija had at last got me alone. 'Why did you do such a foolish thing?' she demanded. 'All the way to Stockholm!'

I sipped coffee, looking across at her. 'They're English.'

She made an impatient gesture. Her eyes were angry.

'Simply because you were determined to do me a favour — or make some sort of gesture.'

'I looked at the map,' I told her, a little annoyed myself. 'The railway's not too far from here. Very soon I could drop you at a station. If that'd suit you better.'

She stared out at Laurie and Cowboy, not prepared to take me up on that. 'They are not couth,' she declared.

I laughed. 'Better go back to Cambridge, Eija. Uncouth.'

'You agree?'

I met her eyes. 'They don't smell. Had you noticed that?'

She grimaced, attacked her omelette, and the mood ran from her. She managed a smile. 'So it was all a story, this about your wife, hah? You suddenly exchange your mind, it seems.'

The second mistake in her so-splendid English; she was rattled. I relented. 'It was all true, and I do no harm in going to Stockholm. If the police are following me, it could help to confuse them.'

Then her hand reached across and fastened on my fist. The fork was immobilised.

'Police?'

I pointed the knife at her. 'The police in the person of an Inspector Richard Kent. He believes she's dead, but he hasn't come right out and accused me of anything.'

Her hand was snatched away.

'Or says he does,' I told her reassuringly. 'It's just words.'

Her eyes were very big. She stuck her

elbows on the table, her fists supporting her chin, as Karin had so often done.

'Is that,' she asked, 'why you have been glancing all the while at your rear-vision mirror?'

She was very shrewd, and did not try to hide her thoughts. I nodded. Outside, Laurie was admiring a Saab Turbo that'd drawn in. He walked round it, kicking a tyre when its owner wasn't looking.

'He was using a red Allegro when he called to see me about Karin and the break-in. But I haven't spotted it behind us. He could have switched cars, of course.'

'There's a lot you haven't told me.' She sounded sad.

'There'll be plenty of time to tell you more, before we get to Stockholm. Come on, let's get going.'

We survived the complex crossovers at Jönköping, and headed north up the east coast of Lake Vättern. This was one of the routes I might have taken to Dalarna. The wind was rocking the car and the rain came down again, even heavier. I was worried about the engine temperature, because the gauge was creeping up. I'd got quite a load on.

Eija had finally reconciled herself to the two lads, turning from time to time to talk to them. Then Cowboy fell asleep, and there was silence except for the thump of the wind gusts against the car.

Around six-thirty I decided we'd best find somewhere to stop the night. The motel signs, which had been frequent between Götebrog and Jönköping, were now far apart. I began to wonder what we were going to do about Laurie and Cowboy.

At last I saw a motel signpost, and turned off at the next crossover. We coasted downhill, the lake barely visible between rock and pine ahead of us, swept round a corner, and found it.

The engine creaked as I pulled in and switched off. It didn't look like a motel to me. I got out to get a better impression, wondering whether I should drive on, and the rain had flashes of sleet in it. The wind caught my breath when I opened the door. Behind a row of petrol pumps to the right, three trailer wagons were parked. Directly in front of me was a wooden-slatted restaurant with a dim light over its porch and a shelter under which a dozen motorcycles leaned on their prop stands. Behind and above it, on the hillside and barely visible behind the slashed curtains of rain, was a row of chalets, painted the red oxide they use so much in Sweden.

'Come on, let's see what they've got,' I said, more optimistically than I felt.

We went inside. It was self-service, with a dozen bare tables, four occupied. It had the lusty warmth of a transport café. The man and woman guarding the counter stood behind an array of hot, tangy food, shouting across the tables in a gabble of Swedish.

'It'll do,' I said. For eating, anyway, I thought.

'*Goddag*,' said the man.

'*Ett snt förskrackligt väder*,' Eija replied.

I thought I understood that. Good-day from the man, and, if *väder* was weather, a comment on it from Eija. *Förskrackligt* just about described it. Then she took over, talking away to him and gesturing towards us. I realised that Laurie and Cowboy were standing silently at my heels. They'd left their gear in the car, and seemed to have nothing to do with their hands without it. Certainly, they were not reaching for money.

Eija had taken control. She ushered us to a table. She sat us down.

'I've ordered four hot meals,' she said, 'and we can get single chalets at a hundred and fifty kroner each.'

That was around £15. I flinched. I wondered again about our two friends, and glanced at them. Cowboy's nose was quivering, as though he was about to cry.

'Care is taken of the meals,' said Eija, not looking at them.

Laurie got the meaning of that. 'We can afford to eat.' Not with much conviction.

She shook her head, and got up to fetch two of the meals when the proprietor shouted they were ready. I followed her quickly and took another tray from the rack.

'They can't afford a room here,' I whispered.

'And we cannot offer to pay. That Laurie is a proud man.'

'Well, what — '

'I don't know.'

We ate magnificently, and afterwards Eija collected two keys at the counter. 'One for you,' she said, making it quite clear. 'And one for me.'

We went out into the storm, with more sleet in it now, all four of us piling back into the car. I drove round, and up the slope to the chalets. They were semi-detached, and small, the upper, unsurfaced path running along behind the row of them. Three cars were already parked further along, and a couple of motor cycles at the far end. Our chalets were numbers 9 and 10. I stopped the car in front of them, switched off, and turned my head.

'What about you two?'

They were shadows in the gloom, though official sunset wasn't due for over two hours. Cowboy glanced at his friend, and for a moment I even thought of offering them the use of the car. But I knew nothing about them.

Laurie said: 'We'll make out.'

'It's terrible out there,' I said.

'We'll manage!' He was savagely controlled.

There was nothing more I could do. I shrugged. 'Well anyway, leave your stuff inside the car. I'll lock it up.'

Eija got out her side and ran for the porch of number 10. I reached across and locked her door. Cowboy slid out from behind me and I pressed down the rear door button. I couldn't reach Laurie's.

'Push the button down and slam the door,' I told him, and saw his arm slide inside. I stood, the keys tinkling in my hand. He slammed the door.

'See you in the morning.' I felt miserable and useless.

'Spot on, mate,' said Laurie.

'But you can't — '

'There'll be cover . . . somewhere.' And Laurie turned away.

I went and took my key from Eija. She opened the chalet door of number 10 and

81

went inside. I opened mine.

I had a tiny toilet with washing facilities, a wardrobe, a small TV set — and two beds. I flung off my coat and tore my tie free, and had a sudden idea. It appeared we'd paid for double rooms, and if I shared with Eija . . . I get these abrupt and splendid thoughts.

I turned to run and shout for the two chaps, and she was standing in my doorway.

'No,' she said gently, closing the door behind her. 'I would like to talk, Owen. And you cannot really have them in here with you.'

As I couldn't explain that I'd thought of it differently, I said nothing. I went to the window. The lake was not visible through the rain. The curtains were thin, but I drew them. Then I sat on the edge of one of the beds, ready to listen, but Eija could not keep still. Karin had been vital, but she had always talked and listened with an immobile concentration. Eija was restless.

'There was no mention of the police,' she decided to say, to lead me in.

I flapped my pockets to locate my pipe. 'I didn't know you well enough.'

'But you do now. I do not like to hear of this.'

Her severe attitude had upset me. 'Because you think I've involved you, is that it?'

'*Miksi sinun täytyy olla niin hankala?*' she clattered out, then she admonished herself with a click of her tongue. 'Why do you deliberately misunderstand me, Owen?'

Because I'm on the defensive, I thought. And anyway, it was my business, not hers. 'I'm sorry. This Kent, the man I mentioned, came to my bungalow when I had the break-in, and he obviously knew something about Karin that he wouldn't tell me.'

'And that is why you must find her, to find out the truth?'

She saw everything as uncomplicated. 'Not just that. She's my wife.'

She had lifted my keys from the bedside table and was slapping them, chink-chink, in her palm, and damn her, those eyes held the same quiet contemplation that Karin's would have done. I'd liked having her with me because she rested me from thoughts of Karin. Her hair had come free in the press of the rain. With a gesture that was also Karin's she swept it back with her hand.

'Then you love her very much?'

'I told you that.'

'It's what a husband would say.' She nodded, having found a niche for the thought.

I shrugged.

'But now I see it is true.' Her head came

83

up. The thought was thrust aside. 'So it was necessary to mislead your Richard Kent, and convince him you are really on holiday, and with your plans very . . . movable — '

'Flexible.'

'Thank you.'

'I don't know what you're trying to say.'

'It is not pleasing to find you have used me — and your two busking friends, yes — to mislead him.'

'That isn't true, and you know it.' She was waiting, my keys, cupped, forgotten in her palm. There was pain in her eyes, and I didn't want to hurt her. I laughed, but not successfully. 'You make too much of it. All right — so I'm impulsive. I do things without thinking them through. But I never thought of it as a blind for Dick Kent. We're old friends — sort of. We play word games with each other, rather like chess, and an advantage here and there falls either way.'

'You're like a little boy, not understanding what's going on around you — ' She was clearly happy to see it that way.

'Nothing of the sort,' I protested.

'You say that you make gestures, like a boy strutting . . . yes? . . . attracting attention. I understand you now, Owen Tanner.'

'Oh, for God's sake!'

'This . . . this Karin affair . . . it is

84

something that confuses you, so you persuade yourself with romantic dreams that it is a quest, you said. An adventure. And you must make gestures, throwing your favours around . . . ' She was calmly cutting me down to size.

But how *could* I have driven past and left them trudging in the rain?

'You don't have to go on,' I said angrily.

She was considering me with her head cocked, amused, even protective. It was maddening. 'They should lock you away, Owen. You must spend your life getting into situations you cannot release yourself from.'

'All right!' I snapped, thumping the bed furiously with my hands. 'With Laurie and Cowboy it was a gesture. I don't know what got into me, but I was sorry for them.'

'There, you see, I was right.'

'For heaven's sake don't keep on being right. Because you're not. Don't include yourself — there was no gesture there.'

That silenced her. She looked at me seriously for a second, then went to the window quickly and peered through the curtains. I wasn't supposed to see her face just then.

She turned back to me. It was the face

I knew, somewhat serious, but with fun in her eyes.

'And what was it, if there was not a gesture, Owen?'

I'd had time to think it out, and wasn't pleased with the answer. She'd been the very antithesis of Karin, at a time when thoughts of Karin meant nothing but confusion. She had been my excuse for not driving like a mad thing directly to Dalarna, because something threatening had entered into it. She was standing there, a living accusation. Eija was the proof that I'd been purely and simply afraid.

'Just you,' I said.

'And what does that mean, just me?' she asked.

'It's pleasant being with you, looking at you, even disputing with you like this.'

'Are we disputing?'

'You disapprove,' I reminded her, 'of me. What I am. I can't help that.'

'I don't disapprove.'

'The lads — '

'If it was a gesture, it was a splendid one.'

That forced me to my feet. She could be infuriating. 'Disapproval dripped from you,' I reminded her.

'No.' She touched my cheek. 'Disappointment, perhaps.'

'I don't understand. I just don't understand a bloody thing.'

'Then — as well as being a stupidly romantic idiot — you are also very blunt, Owen. Not sharp,' she tried. 'Obtuse, yes? You told me how much she meant to you — this Karin of yours. You told another woman that your wife is the centre of your whole being. No man is fool enough to do that unless it is true, and fills his mind. But you did. I admired you for it. And then you seemed to toss it aside for a gesture, and abandon this glorious quest of yours . . . and I was very disappointed.'

I turned away from her. 'It wasn't like that.'

'Then how was it?' she challenged.

'I had to have time to think it out . . . what I was going to do.'

'And what have you decided?'

I hadn't decided anything, but she was forcing decision on me. 'To go on . . . I suppose.'

It wasn't exactly what she'd meant. She seemed to slide off onto another topic. 'This Karin of yours . . . ' I wished she wouldn't use that phrase. Everybody was mine. 'This Karin, would she have approved?'

'Of what?'

'That you'd allow yourself to be diverted,

and make extravagant gestures?'

'Good Lord, no. Very practical, Karin.'

'Then don't you think you should be practical and go to Dalarna, and find out what it is you want to find? She wouldn't expect you to carry around a couple of bearded . . . gentlemen.'

So that was it. She wanted me to dump Laurie and Cowboy.

'Is that what you'd advise?'

She bit her lip. I was still too blunt for her. 'There has been talk of something illegal, even talk that she could be dead. Why should I want you to head into that?' She smiled. 'Alone,' she added, making it as plain as she could.

I played dim. 'You'd prefer me to go back home?'

She shook her head angrily. 'What does it matter what I want!'

Then I saw something in her eyes that explained all the circuitous probing. I saw it, my heart leaping, and I had to reject it. 'I've got to find her. You're forcing me into taking it seriously. All right, so I'll head for Dalarna in the morning.' I paused. 'Alone.'

The keys clattered into a corner of the room. 'I can't talk to you any more!' she cried.

But she *had* made me think of it seriously. 'You're best out of it,' I said. I didn't intend to say it harshly, but that was the way it came out. Nobody ever allowed me to do things my own way, and suddenly she was another complication. 'In the morning we can keep going north. Örebro. I saw it on the map. We'll put you on a train at Örebro.'

I was hurting her. I watched myself doing it, listened to myself. She was unmoving, with no life in her face. But sometimes you have to force the break.

'Hallsberg,' she said tightly. 'The junction is at Hallsberg.'

I hesitated. There was a familiar ring to that name. Hallsberg. But no, it wasn't quite true; the bell was slightly cracked.

'Very well, Hallsberg. Then, perhaps, you'll allow me to head on north.'

'And your two friends?' she jerked out. 'You promised them Stockholm.' And she'd as good as asked me to dump them!

I waved my hand, dismissing the problem. 'Then I'll put them on the train, too. It's over halfway to Stockholm. I'll pay their fares, damn it, because I made them a promise.'

'And pay mine too?' she asked, her voice icy.

'I'll get your cases out of the car,' I said,

on my way to the door, returning to rescue my keys.

I went out into the rain, and nearly wrenched the boot lid from its hinges. By God, I'd got a way with women! She waited in her chalet for me to dump her cases at her feet.

'You are a fool, Owen Tanner,' she whispered. Her voice wasn't steady.

I went back into my chalet, slammed the door behind me, kicked off my shoes, and flung my keys after them, watching them disappear into one of the toes. The memory of Eija's last words wouldn't leave me alone.

Then I lit my pipe at last and flung myself on my back on the bed, and had to confront another change in my lifestyle. It is not possible, flat on your back, to smoke a pipe. Cigarettes, yes. A pipe, no. Irritably I laid it on the tiny stand beside the bed, and lay, staring at the patchy ceiling. I attempted to make sense out of my life, and the women who tried to order it for me. But there'd be time, before we reached Hallsberg . . .

Then presently — because the light was still on when I woke — I must have drifted into sleep. I'd have expected nightmares, but there was nothing until I was jerked awake by a pounding on the door.

I was confused, staggered from the bed, and stumbled for the door. Light was filtering through the curtains. The pounding continued as I reached for the door key, discovered it wasn't there, then found that the door was unlocked. I pulled it open, and Kent thrust past me into the room. I turned, following him, searching wildly for my wits. My heart, provoked by his urgency, was racing.

'What is it?'

He had his back to the light. Now there was no more pretence that he was on holiday. His suit was formal, his stance severely official.

'We've found your wife's car.'

I took two deep breaths. 'Where?'

'At a small town called Hedemora. It's nose-down into the mud of a lake, but you can see the number plate.' He cleared his throat. 'Just.'

My eyes blurred, and I had to fight them back into focus. I realised that the sun was well up. Sun's up, I thought. I glanced at my watch. Eyes working now. It was not quite six o'clock. Arms working too. I had to do the normal things, snatch for my shoes and slip my jacket from the chair back. It was a snatch, but in slow motion. I had to hide my face from him, but I couldn't control my voice.

'And . . . Karin . . . ?'

His voice was calm, trying to exercise some control over me. 'It's very muddy there. It's impossible to see inside. They're arranging special lifting tackle.' I raised my eyes. 'The Swedish police,' he explained. 'There's a car outside.'

'I've got my own car.'

'A police car is faster.'

At least he recognised my urgency. I nodded. I couldn't see my keys anywhere. I didn't need them . . . I was being driven . . . it was something to work out. But suddenly my mind had skidded out of control and I had to have my keys. I dabbed my feet into the shoes, and found them.

'My cases — '

'Let's go,' he said.

We came out into the sun. The sky had cleared and it was a splendid day. Just perfect. A Volvo was parked where my car had been, with a bluff, jovial man in a tan linen suit at the wheel. And there was no sign of my Dolomite.

'My car — ' I bleated.

Then I realised. Laurie had managed well enough, after all. He'd carefully left a door unlocked.

'The bastards have pinched my car!' I shouted, and suddenly the control went, and I stood with clenched fists, glaring round for something to hit. 'My car, my car!' I bellowed at the pines backing the driveway, and Kent took my arm, forcing me into the Volvo.

# 5

I crouched in the corner of the rear seat, well away from Kent. The driver coasted the car down the slope and round onto the road, then his foot hit the accelerator, and the car stepped high and fast, the needle running round the dial. The tyres sighed.

To express his composure, Dick Kent said, 'This is Owen Tanner. Detective Chief Inspector Sjöberg, Owen.'

He half turned his head and smiled expansively to express his pleasure, and grimaced to indicate his distress at the manner of our meeting.

'*Angenämt*,' he said. 'I am Lennart.' He flicked a hand, apologising for not being able to offer it.

'Where is this town?' I had forgotten its name.

'Hedemora,' said Lennart Sjöberg. 'It is two hundred and sixty kilometres. North.'

'In Dalarna?'

'A little way into Dalarna, yes.' He appeared interested in the fact that I'd asked.

So I was going to Dalarna after all. Perhaps

94

far enough into it for it to have snowed there, I thought.

Early commuters were beginning to occupy the roads. He put on his siren until we were clear again, and now we were on a throughway. Kent was saying nothing. It was going to be a run of 160 miles.

'It's a long way,' I said, wondering if I could stand it if it went on too long.

'We did it in two and a half hours coming,' said Kent sourly.

'Two and a quarter, returning,' said Sjöberg happily, and chippings flew as we pounded across a bridge, the air howling round us.

'What is this about your car?' asked Sjöberg.

So I told him, and he drove a couple of hectic miles with one hand, whilst he laid-on a trace for it with the mike in his other. Triumph Dolomite, light blue, automatic transmission, and with my treasured tripod on the back seat.

He was asking me about Laurie and Cowboy. Bitterly, I gave him a full description.

Then there was silence in the car, and Lennart Sjöberg settled down to drive. I thought he'd been moving fast, but no. We went faster. Villages streamed behind us in a blast of reflected siren. Mounting and snaking highways in the hills were dismissed with a casual slide on every corner. The Volvo was not conceived with this in mind.

At last I was able to speak normally to Kent. 'Let's have it. Where the car is. Why.'

'We don't know why. There is a turning from the main street of the town, down between a double row of bungalows.' He was speaking calmly and unemotionally, but perhaps that was his concession to kindness. 'At the bottom there's a lake. One end of a lake. The road ends, and to the left it's just a track, round the south end of the lake, and there's a very minor surfaced road to the right, along past the fronts of holiday homes and well back in the trees. There's a tiny landing stage. Or rather, there was. The Mini destroyed it. It must have driven straight down the hill, not deviating. Someone has said they heard the engine, around midnight.'

Droning detail, to soothe me. I noticed his delicacy. Not 'she' had driven, but 'it'. I nodded.

'Midnight? They'd have got it out by now.'

'The landing stage was there because the approach is marshy. They'll need a long reach. A special crane's on its way from

Örebro. They tried wading out, but the mud swirled up. Nobody got a sight through the windows.'

'They could have, by now.'

'No.'

'Could have lifted it by now.'

'No,' said Dick. 'They'll wait for us.'

'Kind of 'em.'

The sun was hot on my right cheek. I slouched further down into the corner, hiding from something, and feeling sick and empty.

We came up to Hedemora, and it was just another small Swedish town. The main road would have bypassed it. We were at the head of a straight and narrow main street, but just before the shops began we turned left from it. Then there were the bungalows Kent had mentioned, with hedges of wild rose and beech. We coasted down the hill, and already I could see the spikey outlines of a crane against the dark water. People stood at their gates, watching us pass, and dogs ran barking. Three police cars were parked just round the corner to the right, and to the left the trees nudged close.

We got out of the car, and the heat hit me. Twin tyre tracks headed across a stretch of grass, straight for the water. The remains of the landing stage reached out through the mud.

I thrust my hands into my jacket pockets, fists now, and walked forward. Dick Kent remained by the car, but Sjöberg went over to speak with the group around the crane. I stood on the bank, my feet sucking into the wet turf.

The rear bulge of the red metal was visible just below the water, that and the British yellow number plate. The Mini was nose down into the mud, with pieces of plank floating around it, and already the frogmen had fixed the chains. Above my head, the crane reached its gantry from the hard surface of the roadway behind. The reeds stirred as a pair of swans glided through them with curiosity.

Sjöberg was at my shoulder. 'We're ready.'

'You don't have to wait for me.'

He touched my shoulder, acknowledging my anger, and made a gesture. A diesel engine throbbed, and the chains clanked, taking up the slack. The swans hissed, and trailed their wakes across the narrow neck of the lake.

It came up with a sucking sound that felt like something being drawn from deep down in my stomach. Mud ran from it and reeds clung to the glass like needles stitching it together. I moved back. The chains creaked, and somebody called out. The Mini swung as it came clear, presenting the driver's window to me.

I started at it. The mud ran from it like scales, and I could see a figure inside, hanging forward on the seat belt. The window was partly open. Slime moved silently; the roar was in my head. I wanted to scream. I saw the defiled blond hair, and then the shoulders, clad in a loud check. Something she had bought . . . I opened my mouth to cry out, but they were swinging it towards me. Sjöberg had his hand on my arm, restraining me gently. I struck him away savagely, running forward as soon as the wheels curtsied down on the grass verge.

Open six inches. Enough for my arm. It was a check jacket, one I knew after all. I reached inside. Nobody stopped me, so I reached, and lifted the head, already, because of the jacket, expecting the handsome, bronzed features of Anders Norgren. Eija had thanked him for me, for both of us. I expected his face, but could barely recognise it as the mud ran down from the tangle of his hair. A pistol shot had shattered the upper part of his features.

I turned and ran through the trees, twisting, and leaning against the pain of a retching that would not materialise. I leaned panting against a tree, but I was dry, leeched dry, my heart choking me.

Lennart Sjöberg stood close, patiently, with a cigarette pack in his hand. Eventually, I found I could accept one. He lit it for me, watching my face.

'I am pleased it is no worse than shock for you,' he said. 'But for me it is unhappiness.'

The cigarette was American. I drew on it deeply. 'You knew him? I met him on the ferry.'

'He was one of my men.' He shrugged. His grimace was rueful. 'He was supposed to be watching you. Following. He would appear to have gone astray.'

I watched him walk away, a jovial man with his shoulders sagging. I trod out the stub with my heel, and when I lifted my head Eija was watching me from the trees.

I moved towards her, but she did not speak. She stood with her hands clasped in front of her, like a solemn child, and there was something in her eyes that reflected my own distress.

'Owen!' she whispered.

She took my hand, then released it quickly. Perhaps it was cold. I shook my head, because there were no words.

'I have a hired car,' she said. 'Come away, Owen.'

'We're a long way from Hallsberg.' A weak effort at indicating my resilience.

She smiled tentatively.

Behind me, Kent said briskly: 'You're not going anywhere, Owen. We've got to talk.'

I thought Eija might slap his face. She spoke stiffly. 'Where?'

'Alone, young lady.' Then, to me: 'I've booked a couple of rooms at a local hotel. Come on. There's nothing for you here.'

No, there was nothing. I looked at Eija. She nodded once, as though I needed her permission, then I moved away, a yard behind Kent's confident shoulders, trying to match his stride.

We did not go to the Volvo. 'We can walk from here,' he said. We skirted the cars, and now that we were clear of the activity, now that the diesel was quiet, I heard the off-beat tickover of a V-twin motorcycle engine. I lifted my head. I'd once owned a Vincent, and the memory was a comfort my mind reached for.

Laurie was sitting astride a water-cooled Honda 500 twin, its exhaust bubbling. He was wearing a crash helmet that partly obscured his face, but it was clearly Laurie, his deep eyes staring out at me with what seemed like hatred. I opened my mouth to shout, but he let in the clutch, the engine roared, and he swung round into an expert 180-degree turn, his feet up before he'd completed it. The front wheel lifted, but he flung it down. Then he raced away between the bungalows.

'What is it?' said Kent.

'Nothing. I'm seeing things.'

'You've had a shock. Come on, keep up. I've got some brandy in my room.'

The hotel was the Gustav Wasa, a small commercial retreat on the high street junction with a side road. We were upstairs on the second landing, my room a small one next to the TV annexe. It overlooked a courtyard, and beneath my window was parked the red Allegro.

I caught sight of myself in the wardrobe mirror, and understood the veiled glance from the proprietress when we'd been introduced. I hadn't combed my hair that morning and I'd flung on my jacket over an open-necked shirt. I was going to have to sleep in the raw. If I was still there, that night.

'You coming?' he asked, sticking his head into my room, and I followed him across the passage, a puppet he was manipulating.

It was larger than mine, and overlooked the side street. I crossed to the window. Quiet, ochre-plastered houses and a small courtyard opposite a set-back building. An elegant streetlamp with three branched globes, and if I angled my view, just a glimpse of a church further along. Dick was standing by a side table when I turned back.

He had it arrayed with bottles, soda water, tonic, lemons. I wondered when he'd managed to set it up.

He brought me a brandy, and read my mind.

'I arrived here at two in the morning. We left at three-thirty, when Lennart realised they couldn't lift the Mini without the crane. I prevailed on the lady . . . ' His eyes went soft, and he actually smirked.

I tossed down the drink.

'We must talk,' he repeated.

'Not now.'

'Really, Owen — '

'Later.'

I stuck the glass in his hand. I had to get away, on my own, for a while. In my room I washed in ice-cold water, every inch of me. Next door I found the shower in the toilet room, and cursed my stupidity. Then I combed my hair and went out into the street. There was no sign of Dick Kent, or of Eija.

I walked, I don't know where, except that I started off in the opposite direction to the lake. I walked, and looked at the church, not seeing it, and tramped every byway. I collected a hamburger and a can of lager at a snackbar and walked with one in each hand, looking for somewhere I could sit.

I came along a path between trees, the surface uneven with gnarled roots, and through the leaves I caught a glimpse of water. It opened out into a cleared space with a bench by the edge of a lake. It could have been the same lake, but there was no sign of police activity. I sat, and a pair of swans (the same pair?) drifted across to have a look at me.

It was so quiet that my thoughts were a clamour in my head. I didn't want to try to sort things out. Maybe Dick Kent would do that when I got back. I wanted only peace, and even there I wasn't completely allowed it.

The swans had drifted to the bank, and solemnly, heavily, the larger one heaved himself onto dry land and advanced on me, hissing. Perhaps it was his bench. A swan, close-to, is very large, and I didn't like the look in his eyes. Momentarily, I glanced behind me to make sure of an escape route, in case he turned nasty.

I saw a shape dodge quickly behind a tree, and at once I turned back. Another of Lennart Sjöberg's followers? It seemed unlikely.

The swan was surveying me with disapproval. I guessed what he wanted and tossed bits of hamburger bun to him. He gobbled them up, pausing only to hiss at his mate, keeping her away from this treat. I finished it, got to my feet, cleaned my fingers on the wrapping, and dropped it along with the empty can in a nearby waste bin. The Swedes are so tidy. Under my eyebrows I saw the movement again. The figure had the general shape and appearance of Laurie.

I ran towards him, and he didn't wait for me. Perhaps he guessed my mood of brooding anger.

So, for ten minutes, the watcher became the pursued. Hedemora was a quiet little town, and we were in an area obviously planned for demolition. Instead of following, he now led, allowing me glimpses of himself from time to time. I hid in the corner of what had been a dwelling, and waited. He showed himself. I ran to the next corner.

It wasn't a corner, simply the last house in that street still standing. A tracked bulldozer stood idle, its attendant at lunch. A Honda V-twin motorcycle with shaft drive was propped amongst the bricks and the slabs of yellow plaster.

I looked round. There was no door in the remains of the end house. I stepped inside. Down the staircase light shafted from a hole in the roof. An arm came round my throat from behind and a hand groped for my left wrist.

'What y' done with my case?'

The voice was hot in my ear, and Laurie's beard spiked my cheek.

I hacked back at his shins, and he was too inexpert to have anticipated it. The breath hissed in my ear, and his arm relaxed enough for me to duck my chin under it. I bit into his wrist, twisted free, and slammed him with a short right into the belly.

He crouched over, hugging himself. 'Bastard!' he croaked. I followed him up, ready, and slid sideways as his foot lashed out. He was off-balance, stumbled, and sat in the ray of sunlight on the bottom stair.

For once he had nothing on his head. His hair was black, long into his neck, and there was a ridge in it from his usual shapeless hat.

'What's this about your case?' I demanded.

He gasped, trying to stand. His eyes were mean. I put a hand against his chest. 'Me wooden box. You know it. Black. It's got the sax and the clarinet in it.'

'And?'

'And y' sloped off in the night with the car. I saw yer, saw it turn out onto the road.'

He was wearing a black zip-up shirt, with a medallion swinging in front of it hypnotically.

'What time was this?'

'You gotta know. Eleven . . . twelve . . . I dunno. Me stuff was in the back.' I allowed him to stand, and he became more confident. The medallion stilled. 'Saw y' through the window.'

'Window? What window?'

He shook his head, and I took a step forward. He held up his palm. 'One o' the chalets. I bust in.'

'You broke into — '

'A bit of wire,' he sneered. 'Easy.'

'I don't know why I troubled with you two,' I said in disgust.

Then his voice suddenly broke, and he wailed, 'And what y' done with Cowboy?'

I stared at him. He was lost and afraid, and in a corner. He heard the high pitch of his own voice, and it steadied him. I saw the danger in his eyes.

'What about Cowboy?' I asked harshly.

'He was on the back seat.' He whirled his fist furiously in the air. 'The berk! Wouldn't come in for a soft bed. Hadda sleep on the back seat, didn' he!'

'The car was stolen,' I said flatly. 'It must've been him pinched it, you fool.'

'Nah!' He shook his head, rejecting it.

'Couldn't stand you, no doubt.'

'No!' he shouted. Then, more quietly: 'He wouldn't do that. He's my brother.'

I couldn't believe it. There was no resemblance, Cowboy big and soft and easy-going, and Laurie gaunt and aggressive. I felt sorry for him. The aggression was a protective barrier. I sighed.

'The police are trying to trace my car. If you want your instruments back — if you want to find Cowboy — then you'll just have to hope they'll find it.'

'Then, mate . . . ' he stabbed a finger towards my chest, ' . . . you'll have me on your tail till they do.'

I turned away impatiently. It was then that I heard movement behind me, from the street outside. A brick moved under a probing foot, then a shadow ran sideways from the sun. I started towards it, and the shadow slid away. Then I stumbled over dust and broken slats, out into the blinding street, just in time to see a man running away from me around the nearest corner. He was slim, not tall. I could tell no more.

I ran, throwing my toes at the ground. Before I reached the junction I heard an engine start, then a dark blue car accelerated hard across the opening. The man had a long nose, I saw through the glass, and a soft, insignificant chin. Beside him, driving, there was a woman. She did not glance towards me. There was a scarf over her head, but I thought there was a hint of blond hair.

I stood. The dust was settling. The hum of the car was retreating.

'Karin!' I bellowed.

Behind me, the bulldozer throbbed into life. Lunch was over. I turned back, but they were already pushing the scoop into the house at the end, and the Honda had gone.

I found my way back by locating the black and gold ball of the church steeple against the sky. The Gustav Wasa was in the same street.

Eija was waiting in the hall. It was like the hall of an ordinary house, the reception being a table on the first landing with a handbell on it.

She had my cases and camera holdall at her feet, and looked quiet and concerned. She was wearing a short blue jacket over a light blue blouse, and paler blue slacks, and looked very trim and poised, as though to contrast my disheveled appearance. I felt gritty and old.

'I brought your baggage,' she said. 'You'll want a change.'

'Thanks. It's good — '

'I told you, but you might not have understood.' Her teeth plucked at her lower lip. 'When I heard about your car, I asked around, and managed to hire one. When you're ready, Owen, I'll be . . . ' she sought for it, ' . . . available.'

'Where are you staying?'

She flicked me a tiny smile. Her lips were very red and soft. She did not reply.

'Are you fixed up somewhere?'

'I'll be all right,' she assured me.

I watched her leave. She wore her hair short at the neck. I decided I liked the style. The door closed behind her with a gentle click.

I went to find Kent, ready to talk and to listen. But first I put on a clean shirt and hung my jacket over a chair. There was a note on the top of my shirts in the case.

*There are many buttons missing, but I did not have time.*

*Sorry. Eija. P.S. You should lock your cases.*

I laughed and felt better, and went across to Kent's room. He was lying on his bed, reading a paperback.

'You wanted to talk,' I said, making it

110

sound as though it was for his benefit.

'I've been waiting for you.' He swung his feet down to the floor. 'Take a seat.' He pointed to the chair, and waited for me to sit, to fill my pipe and light it, and waited too long.

'So why have you been haunting me?' I asked. 'My wife left me, and there was no crime involved.'

'There is now — Anders Norgren.'

'Not *then*.'

'And it's your wife's car.'

'But *then*,' I insisted, 'there was nothing for the police.'

'Oh, but there was,' he corrected me gently. 'There was a robbery, the theft of a necklace — or more correctly the stones from it — from a strongroom. There was also the death of a man during the commission of that offence.'

I was aware that he was watching me carefully. His voice had been precise and even, the phrasing officialese. I was cautious.

'I don't know what you're talking about, Dick. For God's sake, just say it.'

He smiled bleakly. 'You don't? This happened six or seven years ago. Two men and a woman raided this firm, where they had the Tammela Necklace for polishing and resetting. It was intended for display in

Finland's Museum of Art Treasures. Two men and a woman, Owen.'

'So?' But the pipe was cold in my fingers, and my knuckles as white as the bowl.

'What is your wife's maiden name?'

'What's that got — ' I stopped. My cheeks felt like parchment. I licked my lips. 'Bergström. You know that.'

'That was not her name when she married you, Owen. She was not a spinster, she was a widow.' He picked up his book and thumped it down on the pillow. 'Why the hell am I talking like this?' he said, with a show of anger. 'A name. It's nothing. When you met her, she'd just done two years in Holloway prison for her part in that robbery. Her name was then Karin Bergh. Her husband had been Gunnar Bergh, and the second man was Gunnar's elder brother, Niels. Niels Bergh came out of prison just ten days before Karin disappeared.'

I got to my feet quickly, because his eyes were alight with a pallid sympathy, as though it was my due but he nevertheless offered it reluctantly.

'You're saying . . . ' I twisted the stem from my pipe and blew down it, and started again. 'You're saying that these two facts are connected?'

He knew how to make me turn and face

112

him. He waited. I turned, and he was relaxed.

'Which two?' he murmured.

'Niels Bergh coming out of prison and my wife disappearing.'

'Of course they're connected. Those two events, and a third.'

'I'm not accepting there could be any connection between Karin and . . . and . . .' I waved a hand angrily. 'Oh hell!'

'A drink?' He raised his eyebrows. 'Perhaps?'

'Keep your drinks. What the hell's going on here, Dick? I've lived with Karin for four years. I *know* her. This isn't — '

Then his voice was crisp. 'Don't act like a fool. From what I know, Karin Bergh isn't worth your concern.'

'You'd better justify that,' I growled.

'Just stop prowling, and I will. Sit down, man, sit. And you're having a drink whether you want one or not.'

He brought me a whisky and soda. I can't stand whisky, but it was something to hold on to. 'What did you mean — and a third? What third incident? You talking about the searching of my bungalow?'

'Not that. I'll get to it.'

I looked down at my drink, and tried a quick gulp of it. The flow was warm, and I felt comforted.

113

'We know a bit about her,' he said, perching himself on the bed again. 'When she was twenty, she was working for a Probation Officer — the Swedish equivalent — in Stockholm, and Gunnar Bergh was having to report regularly at that time. He was twenty-four, and from all accounts — no, this is all from his brother Niels — from *his* account, Gunnar had a way with the girls, all charm and a soft laugh and . . . oh, there'd been nobody like Gunnar, not ever, according to Niels. So Karin took off with Gunnar, and they were married, then the three of them conducted a series of crimes throughout the southern part of Sweden. Minor stuff. No violence. Mainly robberies, and all based on Gunnar's charm. *He* found out when a decent haul was possible, where and how, and he used his charm to get what they wanted. Karin,' he observed, 'seemed not to mind.'

I cleared my throat. His eyes were on me at once. I smiled at him. Karin had enjoyed life, I told myself, and Gunnar Bergh had charm.

'Until,' he went on, 'it got too hot for them over here, and they shifted the scene to England. They aimed higher. The Tammela Necklace is a national treasure, but I don't think they expected — '

114

'The crime,' I said softly, not allowing him to wander from the point.

His voice became more crisp. 'Three of them. Karin stayed in the van they were using. Gunnar knew all there was to know, and the two men got to the strongroom. I say strongroom, but it was more like a large safe. Gunnar knew the combination, and it was he who opened it up and stood inside to hand out the stuff. The Tammela jewels came out first. They'd been stripped from their settings, and were in a little velvet bag, pulled together with a string . . . '

He paused. I nodded, putting down my glass, and looked round for where I'd left my pipe.

'And then,' he said, 'another character walked into the scene. According to Niels he was big, and he was wearing some sort of a hood. And he had a gun. He'd only been waiting for the door to be opened. He held out his hand for the velvet bag, and took it from Niels. Gunnar was very still, standing inside the strongroom. Then Karin walked in. She must have seen the intruder following them in. And she was carrying a pistol of her own. The man had obviously recognised the odds. He couldn't face three ways, and it turned out later that his gun was a toy. He slammed the door on Gunnar, and the automatic lock spun the tumblers. Only the two of them, then, and one of them a mere woman with a gun.'

'Karin,' I said, 'is not a mere woman.'

He grimaced. 'Mere or not, she fired, and got him in the arm. He dropped the velvet bag and ran for it. Niels shouted for Karin to get going. She just picked up the bag and ran out with it.' He looked away. 'Not, apparently, too concerned about her husband.'

He drew a handkerchief from his pocket and patted his lips, stared at his empty glass, and went to fill it.

'As far as I know,' he said, his back to me, 'they next met in the dock.'

I went and glanced out again, anything not to have to look at Kent. Laurie was leaning against the three-globed lamp standard, watching the hotel. Kent wanted me to speak, so I was silent.

He looked at me through his glass.

'Your wife was picked up a fortnight later in Stockholm. She denied any knowledge of what had happened to the Tammela stones. Niels . . . ' He shrugged. 'Niels didn't know the combination of that lock. All Niels could remember was that four figures came into it. So he started from the beginning, working through the sequence. He was still at it when the boss's personal assistant arrived. She was the only one, barring Hammerstein himself, who knew the combination. When they dragged him away, Niels Bergh was as good as crazy, and his brother was dead from suffocation.' He cleared his throat. 'Niels Bergh got eight years, and Karin got three. With remission, he came out ten days before Karin suddenly — '

'You said that,' I grated. 'Not my Karin. Another woman.'

'It's your Karin, Owen, and you know it.'

I shook my head stubbornly. He sighed. It was then that I noticed how exhausted he looked.

'You've been played for a fool, Owen. That much should be clear to you. She found you — and anybody would have suited her — found you and used you, as an excuse to remain in England as a British citizen. And somewhere to lay her head,' he said, conjuring up visions. 'Somewhere to wait until Niels could join her, and they could come and dig out those jewels from where she'd hidden them.'

I nodded, agreeing, looking into his eyes and refusing to get mad. Except that my mind was scrambling about, recalling how we'd met. One point he was wrong about.

Karin hadn't found me. I'd found her, in a nightclub on my focusing screen, laughing with a big-shouldered layabout with eyes too close and mouth too open.

'It's possible,' I said. 'What you say is just possible. She came here to show him where she'd hidden them, but then she'd have returned to me.'

'If you want to believe that,' he said negligently, sitting on the bed again.

I didn't like that casual response. He didn't really care what I thought or did. I'd been discounted.

'The third thing,' I said abruptly. 'The theft, Bergh's release. That's two. What's the third?'

He reached behind him and rescued a folded newspaper, but for a minute or two held it across his knees.

'These stones, Owen, the famous Tammela jewels — d'you know what they are? Mostly sapphires, a few emeralds, two larger rubies. Eighteenth-century cut, and almost impossible to fence. Worth next to nothing out of their settings. They'd need recutting, and any jeweller in the world would recognise them.'

'So what's the fuss? They've got nothing.'

'Ah . . . but in their settings they're part of the Finnish national heritage. Those

118

settings have been held all these years by Hammerstein's in London, hoping the stones would turn up. When Niels Bergh was released, then they knew they wouldn't. The settings were therefore returned to Finland. And d'you know how jewellers send most of their stuff, the safest way, the only weak spots being the short trip one end, and the delivery the other?'

'I've heard.' I could sense what was coming. Things began to fall into place, and I felt sick. 'By post. Plain wrapper.'

He grinned, and tossed me the newspaper. It was dated a fortnight before. The *Evening News*.

## DARING THEFT
## TAMMELA SETTINGS LOST

This morning, on his way to the local post office, an official of Hammerstein & Co was brutally attacked and his briefcase wrenched from his hand. The only item in it was a package containing the settings of the famous Tammela Necklace. Readers will recall our news item six years ago, when a robbery at . . .

I tossed it back. 'Of all the stupid, incompetent operations — '

'It went according to plan,' he told me calmly. 'Apart from the brutality of the attack.'

'Plan?' I shouted. 'What plan?'

'Don't you ever stop to think, Owen, before you fly off the handle? Not planned by us. Think about it, and it's logical. The Finnish authorities have always been afraid the stones would be split up, Bergh cutting his losses. They reckoned Karin wouldn't do anything while he was inside.'

'She did plenty.'

He smiled, very thinly. 'But . . . with the settings too, Bergh would have his hands on a fortune. They were willing to pay that, so you can see what that necklace means to them. Oh, it's blackmail, true enough, and they went along with it, just to be sure the whole bundle was kept intact. Damn it all, if Bergh'd walked into Hammerstein's and simply asked, they'd have handed him the settings. But all they had to do was put an advertisement in the papers, disguised as a news item, that on such-and-such a day . . . ' He stabbed a finger at the paper. ' . . . *that* day, the settings would be returned to Finland. That was all it needed. No doubt Karin saw it — '

'Leave her out of it!'

'Sometimes I feel like giving up,' he said

angrily. 'You're so bloody childish, Owen. She's in it. They've got both now, settings and stones, and the Finns are only waiting for Bergh to get in touch.'

'It's simply damned illegal.'

'Of course it is. Why d'you think *we're* involved? Why d'you imagine the Swedish police are in on it? We want those stones and settings, and we don't intend Bergh's going to get away with it.'

'Then why,' I threw at him, 'are you following me?'

'Because we lost her. She took off so fast we missed her. You were all we'd got left, Owen. A poor chance, but we had to use it. You seemed to think you knew where to find her — '

'I don't.'

'Then look at it the other way round. Don't stand there staring, Owen, think about it. She could lead you to her. Perhaps she's already started.' He raised his eyebrows.

'And why should she want me?' I asked quietly.

Then, saying it, I realised the meaning behind Karin's phone call. They had the lot — that was true. But there was something else. Had to be. I didn't know what, but no other possibility made any sense. I considered that phone call. First there'd been probing questions . . . had something gone wrong? I wondered. Then the clue of the snowstorm — surely a lead, but deliberately indefinite. It had all been impersonal, until the end, when Karin had cried out for me not to follow that lead, and had attempted to say more. For some reason, *he* had forced her to make the phone call, but *she* had tried to warn me off. There was danger, and she feared for me!

She needed me.

I could have shouted out in triumph, but he was waiting for me, his smile unpleasant.

'By God, and we never guessed!' he said. 'We get too involved with crime, and miss the obvious. It's you, you great, sexy stud. Got something the rest of us envy. She misses you under the sheets, that's what it is.'

I went for him, plunging at the bed. He'd seemed to expect it and rolled clear, and I fell face down on the cover. When I looked up he was balanced on the balls of his feet, the advantage was his, and the brief flash of anger was dead.

'So now you know,' I said.

'All that worry you gave us!' He shook his head. 'And all the while it was the same old stimulant — sex.'

'It was you searched the bungalow,' I said dully, working my way to my feet.

'No. We don't understand that. All we could think was to keep an eye on you.'

'So what's changed? You're trying to use me, is that it? You want me to lead you to her?'

'What's changed is Anders Norgren's death. The odds have gone too high, Owen, and we daren't risk having you involved any more.'

'Leave Norgren out of it, for God's sake!'

'Leave him out!' He threw up his arms. 'I can't believe what I'm hearing. He's dead, Owen. Remember? Murdered, and in your wife's car. We're not playing games any more, it's a manhunt, and you're in the middle. I'm telling you — as politely as I can — you're out of it. Finished. I just want you to turn round and go home, Owen.'

'A lot of talk for that.'

'I wanted you to be sensible. Wanted you to see she's not worth any effort.'

'Anders Norgren,' I said stiffly. 'Tell me about him. What was he doing in Hedemora?'

'You. You, again. You with your tale of phone calls with snow under the edge of the booth.'

'Make sense.'

'These Swedish boys, they dash off and act on their own,' he said bitterly. 'A bit like you. Norgren knew that Niels Bergh was born in this town. And they did have snow — or at least, sleet — in Hedemora that night. He took it into his head to come here. Phoned in that he *was* here. And then . . . nothing. Until they found the car.'

I moistened my lips. My tongue felt thick. 'And Bergh's place?'

'Nothing. It's derelict. They're knocking the whole row down.'

His phone rang, a burr every three seconds. I watched him pick it up, but I didn't try to follow the conversation. My own thoughts were difficult enough to follow. It was an effort to realise he'd hung up and was speaking to me.

'They've found your car.'

'Where is it?'

'Stockholm. Abandoned. It seems it blew a gasket on the way into the city.'

'Then I'll have to go there. It'll put me out of the chase. Bet that suits you.'

'Oh, you'll have to go, right enough,' he agreed. 'Sjöberg's driving you in, tomorrow morning. There'll be statements to make and questions to answer.'

I laughed. 'You bloody cheap fraud, Dick. Questions to which I shouldn't know the answers, but I do, because you told me.

Only you'll deny you did. You'll keep me out of it all right.'

His cheeks were grey, with tiny patches of colour on each high cheekbone. The one thing he hated was being accused of sharp practice.

I said, 'This house of Bergh's — have you been there?'

Surprised, he jerked out: 'Yes. It's deserted. I told you.'

'Take me to it.'

'Now?'

'While it's light. Take me, and on the way . . . I suppose we can walk? . . . on the way you can try to explain how you think you can stop me. I'm here as a tourist. All legal.'

He reached for his jacket. Colour had returned to his face.

'Believe me, Owen, you won't be able to move an inch.'

# 6

We strode along side by side, neither of us speaking. We headed towards the church, passed it, and turned off into a side street, then into another. This was new to me, not the district where I'd encountered Laurie. Casually I turned, using my jacket flap to protect the flame of a match, but I could see nobody following.

'You completely fooled us,' Dick grumbled. 'Waltzing around with a woman and two bearded goons, just as a blind!'

They were a row of squat houses, crumbling, not really needing the assistance of a bulldozer. The exterior walls were painted red oxide, the colour of dried blood. No one was in the streets. It was haunted by no more than memories.

The house he led me into had part of the roof fallen in and cascading down the stairs. It reduced the possible area of interest. We stumbled over bricks and plaster, and dust danced in a shaft of sunlight through a hole in the side wall.

We were in what had been a kitchen, large and square. It had probably also been used as

126

a living room. An iron stove backed against a wall, its surface covered with brick dust and red, flaking plaster. I put my hand to it. Cold.

'We've been here,' said Kent impatiently. 'And glanced in?'

There were footprints in the dust layer on the red-tiled floor. Red . . . red . . . I bent to look at them.

'Courting couples,' he grunted.

I stared back at him. 'The Swedes are more fastidious.'

He flinched, his eyes bleak.

Karin was tall for a woman, which might have attracted her to my five feet eleven inches. She normally wore low-heeled shoes, except for evenings, and I knew her size, small for her height. Her hands had been small too, and delicate . . .

I located a clear print. Neat, compact heels, the sole pattern that of her Polyveldts, which she'd taken with her. I straightened, not commenting, mainly because words would have choked me.

I found the dark stain of dried blood beside the doorway, where a door had been. In the dust on the floor there were scrape marks, as though fingers had scrabbled for just that final second.

Then I could no longer keep it to myself.

He walked carefully round the edge of the room, and looked at the spot.

'I've got to get back and phone Sjöberg,' he said.

'Yes, do that.'

We walked back together. In his room, he made the call. Then he ordered a meal for two to be brought up to his room, there being no dining room, and he talked of other things, reminiscences of our times together in the force. He was making it very clear that he was talking to a man who was no longer involved with Karin and Niels Bergh.

When I eventually went to my own room he did not ask for the key, and then lock me in, but there was a young and athletic man sitting alone in the TV lounge, which was open-fronted, and he hadn't got the set switched on.

I went to my window. I could have climbed out — maybe. I could have stolen his red Allegro — maybe. Control yourself Owen, I told myself. Don't go wild.

My jacket was exactly as I'd left it, my cases sitting as they'd been, but on the tiny dressing table lay my picture of Karin in her folk costume. I hadn't put it there.

It was lying face up. A moustache had been drawn in with ball-point. That was Karin, her sudden bubbling urge to infantile humour in the middle of a time of crisis. She had always been able to shatter my depression with it. I turned it over, and she had written:

*So you found it, Owen. Clever darling. I'm sorry about the car. But you should pursue it.*

Blast her, I could have strangled her if she'd been there. It meant nothing — or everything.

I'd found it! Found what? She had to mean the photograph itself. And . . . which car? Hers or mine? And . . . for heaven's sake, what was I to pursue? Was that a slip of her English, pursue for follow? Pursue an idea, or follow a lead! It meant nothing, damn her. Clever darling! I felt as clever as a physics teacher arguing with Einstein.

But this time there was nothing personal from her, unless I counted 'Clever darling'. The message was strangely cold. If the car referred to was hers, the words: 'I'm sorry about the car' were almost obscene in their cynicism. Sorry I had to leave it with a body in! Then I realised she hadn't been alone in my room. The message was from Niels Bergh. You should pursue it. Why the hell did he want me to pursue it? Meaning the clue of the photograph, I supposed. He had stood over her as she wrote it . . . and there could be nothing personal in it from Karin to me.

By the time I fell asleep I'd worried it into a tangle of emotions, and was startled awake by another of Kent's pounding acts on the door. He told me that after breakfast Lennart Sjöberg would be there to drive me to Stockholm.

We ate in the TV lounge, on low, glass-topped tables. Kent ate fast, in a hurry to see the back of me. I drained the thermos flask of coffee.

Sjöberg was waiting outside, leaning in the sun against the roof of the Volvo, and chatting warmly to Eija in Swedish.

'The young lady,' he said, 'insists on driving you.' He turned to her. 'But you will follow me closely, please.' This, being intended for me, too, he said in English.

The athletic young man in his passenger seat was nearly asleep.

We followed Sjöberg. He drove fast, but not as fast as the day before. With casual ease, not always with her eyes on the road ahead, Eija matched him. A small black dot, which was Laurie on the Honda, never tried to overtake and never fell back. We were leading him to Cowboy.

Eija did not question me, so in the end I told her all that had happened, reading

130

for her the message on the back of the photograph. I held it up for her to take a quick glance at the moustache.

'Your wife has humour?' she asked.

'That sort.'

'You know what I think?'

'Tell me.'

'That your man Kent is quite true . . . correct.'

'I take it that you're not talking about using you as a blind?'

She flashed me a look of angry scorn. Then she smiled.

'You are a dear idiot, Owen, but when you say such things, please do it when my hands are free.'

'I promise.' I wondered what she'd do with them. 'I don't remember Kent being correct about anything.'

'When he warned you to keep out of it.' She suddenly sounded more cheerful. 'And when he made it impossible for you to go on.'

I was silent. She glanced sideways. 'Owen?'

They were all so confident I was out of it. 'You don't understand, do you, Eija! How can I turn back now?'

'But there's danger. There's been one killing.'

'There's more danger this moment if you

don't watch the road.'

'Sometimes,' she decided, 'I think I could hit you.'

Then she told me all about the delights of Stockholm, and about the flat she shared with her friend. 'Lisa is a darling,' she said. 'You would like her.' She pursed her lips at that, then smiled. 'But she is at home so very rarely, and travels the world. She is a stewardess on an airline.'

She had booked a room for me at the Hotel Terminus, opposite the Stockholm Central Railway Station on Vasagatan. She would know, being a courier, where to send people who asked for accommodation. She would be known. The two young ladies greeted her by her christian name at the reception desk, and Sjöberg's man stood politely, waiting. Eija left, waving, but not goodbye. She had written her flat's phone number on the back of her business card, which had a coloured picture on the front of a ship of the Vikinglinjen. Across the top was printed: Konferens-Och Specialresor. Beneath it: Eija Karlsson.

There were two lifts. The young man squeezed with me into the tiny two-person one in the corner. Together we examined my small room, admired the watercolour of pansies on the wall, unpacked my cases, then he took me to the office of Lennart Sjöberg. He didn't ask, just took me.

The building was impressive, but Sjöberg did not intend to impress. His office was untidy and informal. He sat me down and sent for coffee, then quietly, smiling, and with a sharp perceptiveness, he tore my mind to shreds, sifted it, and returned it to me unharmed, even soothed. I did not tell him which parts of my statement had come from Dick Kent, but he did not need telling.

'Your Richard Kent has been indiscreet,' he murmured.

In the end we sat back and waited while they typed my statement. I refused his offer of a cigarette and lit my pipe. I was relaxed, one ankle hooked over the other knee. There seemed to be nothing to fear from Sjöberg.

'I cannot read your intentions, Mr Tanner,' he said, and I stared at him inscrutably, 'but, for your information, let me tell you that Anders Norgren was killed by a six-point-three-five mm bullet. It is an unusual calibre, used in the weapons our own service carries. It is intended to wound, but not kill.'

'This one killed.'

'Fired from very close, and intended to kill.' He thought about that, giving me time to do the same. 'It is a woman's pistol, probably a Walther PPK.'

'But not necessarily fired by a woman.'

'Let us hope not. Ah, here we are.'

They brought me four copies of my statement to sign. I read it — it was in English. I signed, and he gave me one copy to keep. Then the young man drove me back to the hotel. He gave me a piece of paper, on it written the information about my car. It was at a garage called Scan-Auto in Ulvsanda.

'We had it towed to a British Leyland agency,' said my friend. 'It is very close to the Bromme Airport.'

I thanked him, and we shook hands. Then he left me, though I guessed he wouldn't go far.

I rang Eija, and she brought her hire car and drove me out to the suburb of Ulvsanda, where they produced the man who had the English. It was not the head gasket that had blown, but the forward inlet manifold gasket, which carried a waterway to the thermostat. This technical information we fought our way through over the turmoil of jets taking off.

'Difficult to obtain,' he said, shaking his head, meaning the gasket.

I told him that I believed that Saab had used the same engine in 1972.

'This we are knowing,' he said. 'Our man

'as driven to the agency.'

'And how long — '

'Two days, if all is okee.'

I looked at him with suspicion. He smiled. 'Your car, it 'ad been driven very strong.'

He meant hard. I asked if I could see it, and he took me through into the workshop. They had a large part of my engine spread on a bench. There was no tripod inside the car, and no black box belonging to Laurie. I thanked him, and Eija drove us back into the city.

'And now,' she said, parking the car in a pay-and-display slot opposite the Grand Hotel, 'we have lunch, and then I will show you Stockholm.'

So now I was a tourist, as I'd claimed to Kent, to be delighted by her beloved city on the water. She would listen to no protests, and after all, what else could I do? What else, and enjoy it so much?

The air in Stockholm seemed clean and fresh. It was another fine day, and we strolled along the quayside, looking at the shipping. She said I must see Kungsträdgården, the King's Park, so we walked there, stood and watched the chess game, being played with two-foot-high pieces on a chequered board as big as my lawn, were sprayed by the multiple fountain at the far end, and sat on the

135

benches to watch the people of Stockholm lounging in the sunlight they loved. They sat back, faces raised to it, eyes closed. We found a table outside the café-restaurant and drank lager and orangeade, with sandwiches, and watched the sparrows feeding their young on crumbs left on the next one.

I felt a lethargy creeping over me, lulled by the beat of the fountain. In this setting, surrounded by the vivid splashes of geranium red and the blue and yellow of pansies, it was difficult to imagine that evil could exist, or that danger need not be so very far away.

'I must get back to the hotel,' I murmured.

'But why?'

'A shower. A change of clothes. I haven't shaved for two days.'

'But you look beautiful! So . . . informal. And your beard — in a week you'll be a viking.'

I grinned. 'And take up raping and pillaging?'

'What,' she asked, 'is pillaging?'

And, strolling along the busy Hamngatan, past the big stores, we paused at the end to stare at the huge circular fountain that formed the traffic island, with the glass tower in the middle. We strolled along the upper stage of the sunken area, which Eija told me had the Tunnelbana central station beneath.

There was a wide run of steps at the end, people sitting on them in the sun, and a woman selling something from a tray hanging from her neck. Softly, filtered through the pedestrian chatter on the still air, I could hear the lilting tune of St James Infirmary Blues, played on a saxophone this time.

I began to run. Now I could hear the bass beat of the guitar. I rounded the corner, clutching the railings to steady me. In front of me was the fall of wide steps down to the chequered pavement of the lower level. They sat on the fourth step from the top, their backs to me, their audience a scattered group who sat and stood around them. Cowboy's black plastic guitar cover was spread to receive the contributions from appreciative fans, and his face was raised, a smile of pleasure on it, bobbles swinging from his bush hat as he nodded to the rhythm.

I tossed a ten-kroner note between them. It fluttered down between Laurie's feet. One of his deep, dark eyes swivelled at me beneath a bushy eyebrow, and the blues faded to grey, then died into darkness.

'What the hell've you done with my tripod?' I shouted.

There was a muttering around us. People began to drift away. Cowboy rubbed his face unhappily, and slowly he got to his feet.

'Now . . . well . . . you know . . . '

I didn't know. I told him so. I pointed out that *he* knew, and he was going to tell me, or I'd accomplish obscene rites with his guitar. Our audience began to learn a few new English phrases.

'He's gotta eat, mate,' said Laurie uncomfortably.

'Are you telling me he's pawned it?' I demanded, sticking a fist beneath Laurie's nose.

'Not pawned,' Cowboy said miserably. His eyes were level with mine, but he was standing one step lower.

'You sold it!' I cried in anguish.

He backed another step, and Laurie grabbed my arm in agitation. 'He can't play on his own. Don' you see! He'd have starved. He's only got four chords.'

Cowboy was a long way from starving. Health and vitality shone in his plump cheeks above the immature beard.

'Take it easy,' he muttered.

'All right,' I said heavily. 'You sold it. So you're going to show me where, and now, right now, before I lose control and kick you right up the taters.'

Cowboy said he'd show me. 'Only a bit of a way,' he said, as though that might appease me.

I leaned down and snatched up the ten-kroner note, and, turning, saw that a police car had drawn up across the street behind me. The door opened and the driver got out. She was a tall blonde with long legs in their dark blue slacks, a peaked cap on the back of her head, and one of the pistols Sjöberg had mentioned nestling in a holster on her hip. Her bearded mate sat quietly in the car. Eija walked up to the blonde, and began to speak quietly to her.

'We leave,' I said to Cowboy, 'now.' I turned, as Laurie began to nest his sax. 'Not you, friend. You wait here.'

It was in the same street as my hotel, farther up, where the shops slipped a couple of notches in status and grubby hotels presented no more than a narrow door to the pavement. We passed two camera shops. The third had its windows packed with second-hand items.

'There it is,' said Cowboy proudly.

My tripod! 'How much did he give you?'

'Fifty kroner.'

Five quid! It'd cost nearly a hundred. The ticket on it asked for 600 kroner. 'I am going to kill you, Cowboy,' I told him before I went inside.

There was some difficulty. I told the proprietor that it was my tripod, and he wasn't going to get 600 kroner out of me. He shrugged, benign and implacable. I told him that no less than a Chief Inspector of Police could verify that it had been stolen from me, and he became less benign. Also a British Inspector, I said, adding the magic, though untrue, words Scotland Yard. He flinched. I mentioned that a friend of mine was, at that very moment, speaking to an officer in a patrol car. I got it back for forty kroner, and felt so good about it that I decided not to kill Cowboy.

I had no chance to give him this news, because he had gone. I walked back to the Drottninggatan Steps, where Eija was waiting for me.

'They went away,' she said. 'Very fast.'

I grunted. 'And the police?'

'I spoke to them. I explained, and they were very sensible.' She looked at me, her nose crinkling. 'There was no gun-play. No shots.'

I grinned, and hefted my tripod.

'And it is this,' she asked, 'has caused all this upset? You frightened them, Owen.'

'I hope so. Yes, this is very precious. Karin gave it to me.'

'Ah!' She linked her arm in mine. 'And now . . . we look at the shops?'

'No. I really want to go back to my hotel.

Can't I meet you later?'

She agreed, and it was what we did. We arranged to meet by the lake. 'At the bottom end of Vasagatan,' she said, 'and the other side of the traffic.' When I got there the gentle evening was resting on the water, and she was leaning over the rail, watching it. One delightful hip was hitched higher than the other in light fawn slacks, and she was wearing another of her blue, short jackets. Like a uniform. She turned, sensing my presence, smiling. The sun was warm on her cheeks, and picked out flares of copper in her hair. There were flowers embroidered on the collar of her white blouse, their bloom in her eyes. She was smiling. I could have kissed her. I did. Her lips tasted of sweet, desperate longing, and I already had more trouble than I knew what to do with.

She took my arm, her other thumb hooked in the strap of her shoulder bag.

'Owen, I am going to take you to a small restaurant I know, and we shall eat Swedish.'

We crossed the water, using the Vasabron bridge. She glanced at me. 'It is very peaceful. Yes?'

I said, yes it was. Distantly, a ship hooted, and somewhere in far waters a motor boat howled away into silence.

We walked up into Gamla Stan, the old town that includes the Royal Palace. It seemed to be her happy hunting ground.

'They will be changing the guard. Do you wish to see that?' she asked.

'Not now.' I could hear martial music, somewhere way over to my left. I did not wish to become aroused.

The street we were mounting was cobbled. Yellow ochre facades glowed in the evening light, but here, the buildings being high and close together, the shadows were already lying in doorways and in the narrow side streets. She turned up one of these and it became an alleyway. Silversmiths advertised with wrought-iron signs poised over our heads, and we lingered in a tiny, set-back square, with boxes of geraniums and a bronze statue of two men boxing. We emerged at the top under a lowering arch, into a street where the strollers were more numerous, and it was possible to view the window displays of shops each side by walking down the middle.

'This is Västerlånggatan,' she said. 'This is where all the buskers come in the evening.'

I could hear that. They spaced themselves at thirty-yard intervals, but all the same you could always hear two at the same time. A pallid youth was seated in a doorway, playing the guitar better than he could sing. A tall old man was playing Bach on a violin. A trio of guitar, double bass and flute were playing around with Scarlatti, and only one couple were offering straight pop. One of them was a girl. I think. Further down, Laurie and Cowboy were well into a jumpy piece I recognised as belonging originally to Scott Joplin.

They had a small crowd around them, and Laurie noticed us, flying at once into hectic variations. Cowboy fixed me with apprehensive eyes, but missed only one of his four chords.

I was feeling good. I put back the ten kroner I reckoned I owed them, and Eija squeezed my arm. Then we went to sample her restaurant.

She was correct about its being small. Its door was low; the window would not have replaced my car's windscreen. From outside it was a dark cavern, sparked here and there with dim red lights.

'Come on,' she said.

They had packed in a hundred tables. Each one had a little red glass with a nightlight in it. If you put your elbows on the surface, there'd be no room for cutlery. A great noise of champing and Swedish conversation surrounded us. I wasn't sure which was which. Eyes caught a spark here

143

and there. Eija clambered to a table for two in a corner, and a waiter climbed over the intervening shoulders to take our order.

We had the wine of the day that wouldn't have lasted until tomorrow, and food which I couldn't really see but tasted of heaven, if they have fish in heaven, and cream and paprika and spices I'd never heard of, and they brought us coffee with a haunting bouquet. We had brandy. Our knees were locked together, and her scent was a delicate tracery beyond which I saw nothing but Eija.

We left. The narrow street seemed a vast expanse in which I wanted to run and skip.

The twilight lingered. The strollers were still there, the buskers still busy. But there was no sign of Laurie and Cowboy. We climbed again, up a narrow alley with no pavement.

'We're coming up to Stortorget,' she said. 'That's the square in front of the Börshuset, the old town hall. There was a terrible massacre there, around 1600, and they say the blood ran down this street like a river.'

'Pleasant,' I said.

We emerged into Stortorget. There was a sound of weird music, which immediately attracted my attention. A group of youngsters in simple smocks and green or red stockings were rehearsing a mime play. They had a crimson stream of velvet strewn down the Börshuset steps and across the cobbles into the centre of the square, and were dancing and singing a strange, passive rondelay in two files, one each side of it.

'The carpet,' said Eija, her breath soft in my ear, 'represents the blood. They are chanting a solemn lament.'

Two boys sat on the steps playing medieval instruments, one an ancient hurdy-gurdy with a handle and a finger board with strings; the other a primitive accordian with paper bellows and a reedy throat. Behind them, deep in the shadows of the doorway, a third lad had a very modern set of drums, though their rhythm reached back into time.

The dancing stopped. Their director, who might have been eighteen, clapped her hands, pointed and cried out instructions, and they took their positions again. Quietly, on benches or standing back as we were, the critical audience watched.

'It is their midsummer play,' Eija told me. 'They are very serious — to get it right.'

Near the corner of the building there was standing a man whom I knew. I had last seen him in Hedemora, when he'd run for his car and been driven away by a woman I'd thought to be blonde.

I turned my back on him quickly. Eija made a slight sound, as her arm was drawn from mine.

Karin was walking towards me across the square.

I made a slight sound, too.

# 7

I had known exactly what I would say to her. The questions were stacked conveniently in my mind, ordered into degrees of importance, and I had even imagined the calm way I would put them, reasonably and coherently. I had visualised the setting, but this was nothing like it.

Panic flooded me when I realised my mind was blank, and only a second, perhaps, remained to recall it. She stood. Her eyes were startled — afraid? I couldn't tell. The light was dim. She lifted her head. The hand that had flown to her face, perhaps in a belated attempt to hide her identity, now fluttered towards me. She seemed as locked in uncertainty as I was myself. The gesture could have been towards Eija, in appeal.

I managed to croak, 'Karin?' I couldn't suppress the query in my voice, questioning her surprising and abrupt appearance. I tried to move towards her, then clamped down on the effort in case it startled her.

'Karin, let me speak,' I whispered. The music behind me hissed and creaked. I saw now that she was entreating me, her lips quivering, pouting to form what could be intended as 'Please!'

Bodily, she thrust herself away from me with a small sway backwards, as though I'd launched a blow at her. Then at last she managed to speak, but her eyes were not on mine. She was staring beyond my shoulder, and I saw horror there.

'Please . . . Owen — '

Then she half turned, poised to run.

'Wait!'

She snapped one look at me of warning or of dread. 'Do not . . . oh, Owen, do not go north.'

Then she'd begun running, back the way she'd come. Behind her, facing the Börshuset, was an imitation British pub with outside tables. It cast a dim light, across which she ran. She was heading to the right of it, where there was a comforting darkness, heading into an echoing, empty street that sloped away from us. I gave a shout, and my legs ached into movement with a burst from tension.

But she'd gone into clattering full flight. Here there were cobbles, and they threw my ankles, the light only the poor glow of a few widely-dispersed wall brackets. The sky-glow was high and narrow. I ran onwards, downwards. Karin was pitching from side to side, searching for escape, but there were no side turnings; the wall surfaces each side were blank. Then there was a dark church, looming up on my left. I paused, stopped. Her retreat sounded to the right, and then, when I plunged again, there were people around, staring behind them down a narrow, sweeping lane, and still there were no side turnings. I saw her in the distance as a flitting shadow, and pounded in pursuit. It curved away to the left. I had a sense that it was widening, the echoes changing.

But the echoes were deceptive, our own clattering heels mixed with others. I heard my name shouted, but it seemed to come from all round me, swirling about my head. Then pounding footsteps were at my heels. Karin had curved away from my sight for a moment. A panting that was not mine was in my ears. I flicked my head round. Darting shadows.

Karin stumbled. I felt rather than heard her cry of distress as she fell. She was within my grasp. I'd take her shoulders, and she would listen to me and tell me what I wanted to know.

A weight caught my left shoulder. I stumbled sideways and missed a step. My hand went out to the wall on my right, but there was no wall, just a blank emptiness, and the tackle became firm and urgent. I was over, toppling, then fell rapidly.

There are thirty-four steps down the steep and narrow Mŕten Trotzigs Grand. Later, I counted the bruises. There was nothing my flailing arms could cling to in order to halt me. The steps are four feet wide, butting onto blank walls. I fell, rolling and panting, shouting out in pain and anger, and I do not remember when I stopped.

Cowboy was bending over me. We were a few yards from the bottom end of the lower street, the busker's paradise, but here no buskers came. It was quiet, the light poor, but I could see the sweat of concern on Cowboy's face.

'Eh then,' he whispered. 'You all right?'

I tried to move. What had been a whole body creaked into twisted pain. I panted from the effort.

'I think something's broken.'

'Lie still, then.'

'Help me sit against the wall.'

Grunting and groaning, we made it that far, which meant my back wasn't broken. My feet were against the opposite wall, my knees bent. My body was operating, but my head still swam. I ached from shoulders to thighs.

'What happened?' I asked, and my voice

was dangerous, I knew, because I had lost Karin.

'Laurie pushed you down the steps.'

'Laurie . . . *what?*'

He looked at my locked fingers on his wrist. 'A feller took a shot at you. Laurie barged you outa the way before he could do it again.'

I released his arm slowly. Things were crawling in my belly. He grinned, a lost child, tentative.

'Heh . . . you need a bodyguard.'

I stared at him. He was big, strong and naive. 'You?'

'We was watching out for you. There was something — you know — somethin' you was walkin' into. Then there was this guy . . . and the woman came up to you. The guy walked nearer. He'd got one hand in his pocket. Laurie knew — '

'Laurie's been watching too much telly,' I said moodily.

'All the same . . . It was Laurie moved first, and I *saw* the gun. I saw it, Mr Tanner, in this feller's hand.'

'Yeah . . . sure.'

'Then you was all running down the alley, and I had to dump our stuff and run after you.' He paused, glanced up into the tunnel of the steps with concern. 'He knocked himself out when he hit the wall. Laurie did.'

I saw his anxiety. 'Then go and see how he is.'

He scrambled eagerly from his crouch. 'Now don't you move.'

Move! 'What, and lose my bodyguard!'

He scrambled up the steps. I watched him go. Then it was quiet, and Eija hadn't come. I didn't dare to think of Karin, so I thought about Eija. But she was not there.

They came down one after the other, humping their kitbag, the black case, and the guitar. Laurie's hat was in his hand. He bent to unload, and the livid bump shone just below his hairline.

'You okay?' I asked.

He ignored the question. 'There's a bullet hole in the wall up there.'

'Then you saved my life.'

'It was high. He fired to miss.' Laurie dismissed it.

But Cowboy said eagerly: 'We owed you one.'

'Pay the balance, then, by getting me to my feet. The police'll be here any minute.'

'Nah!' said Laurie. 'I hung around. It's quiet up there.'

It was not quiet where I was. My ears were roaring, and my head was pounding with the desperation in Karin's voice. For the moment, I could not recall the words she'd used, only their tone.

'All the same, help me up, or I'll set solid.'

They helped me up. Laurie said there was blood running down my face. I touched it, and it was sticky. They half carried me into the slightly better light of the bottom end of Västerlnggatan. To our left was an open square, and I caught a glimpse of water — the river or the lake. I sat on a low wall. My pipe was in two pieces, the stem broken.

'You got a cigarette?'

Laurie looked disgusted, but Cowboy produced a crushed pack, in which was one cigarette. He glanced in guilt at Laurie as he offered it to me. I drew at it desperately. And still Eija had not come.

'All the same, we owed y',' said Cowboy. His nose, I realised, had the same acquiline thrust as Laurie's. There were creases in the corners of his eyes. Neither of them was as young as I'd thought.

'For pinching the bloody car,' I decided to say.

Cowboy was spreading his palms. 'Nah . . . well . . . '

'Tell me,' I jerked at him. 'Laurie's already said you slept in it.'

'Yes. Well . . . he left the door catch up f' me. So I got down on the back seat, see. It makes yer knees ache. And then she came and got in the front.'

She? But I didn't say it.

'She musta let the brake off, 'cause we rolled down the slope, and the engine caught at the bottom, and then she drove like bloody hell, and it scared the life outa me. I kept me head down. O' course. She musta thought I was luggage or somethin'. But man . . . she moved. Y' know. She din' half push it, an' it went on and on.'

Easily three hours, I'd have guessed.

'An' then we stopped. She just got out and walked away. I give her time, see, to get clear, then I got out and looked round. It wasn't dark. Sun was nearly showin', and steam was comin' outa your bonnet like nobody's business. There was a park or somethin' right next to us, so I unloaded Laurie's stuff and mine — '

'And the tripod,' I said. 'Don't forget the tripod.'

'Yeah . . . the tripod. I'll pay yer back, Mr Tanner. We done well tonight. Look — '

'Tell the man,' cut in Laurie, not prepared to discuss finance.

'There's nothin' else to tell. I kipped down in a shelter f'r a coupla hours, then walked into Stockholm. We was only a mile out when the car packed in.'

Laurie spoke sourly. 'You wanta watch that bird y're latchin' on to.'

I jerked my head at him.

'This Eija something. She's runnin' you around, mate. Drove your car away in the night, didn't she.'

'It was Eija?' My voice was difficult to handle.

'Who d'you think? Cowboy saw her. No mistake.'

Then she chose to come at last, round from the quay and striding unconcernedly towards us.

'Owen?' she called.

Her stride lengthened, quickened, until she was running.

'*Voi hyvä Jumala* . . . I've searched . . . Your face! Can you stand? You're hurt,' she said accusingly.

'You searched the wrong alley. I've had time to recover.'

'You poor darling. I was delayed by the police. I had to do much talking.'

She was good at talking to the police. 'And what did you tell them?'

She shrugged. Laurie and Cowboy had

155

retreated into the background. They could not see her tiny grimace of distaste.

'I said you were drunk. The English public house gave me the idea. I said you were drunk, and chased a woman down Skomakargatan. I needed to speak quickly.' Talk fast, I guessed. 'Drunkenness is an offence, Owen,' she told me severely, as though I had, indeed, been drunk.

She reached out, shook my arm for my attention, tenderly touched my face, and drew in her breath when I winced. She didn't ask about my guts, which were swirling, and I hung on tenaciously to that splendid dinner.

'You two,' she said, turning to my bodyguards, 'stay here. I am going,' she told me, 'to get a taxi.'

She walked snappily away.

I looked at Laurie and Cowboy. Neither was happy. Laurie flapped his hat against his thigh.

'This looks like goodbye, fellers,' I said. 'Reckon we part even.'

'Y' need a bodyguard, Mr Tanner,' said Cowboy. I wondered whether he was thinking about Eija.

'There's no way she's going to let you load yourselves into the taxi,' I said. 'It's goodbye, and thanks for the . . . diversions.'

'We'll be around,' said Laurie.

They loaded up, and like miserable shadows they faded into the night. I looked after them and nearly called them back, but Eija arrived with the taxi.

'Here.' She put a hand under my arm. 'Let me help you.'

'I can stand.' An exaggeration.

She called something in Swedish to the taxi driver, who came to help her. I felt like a shattered old man. Every inch of me protested as I straightened. I saw that Laurie's hat lay at my feet, and I folded it quickly, stuffing it into my side pocket. He'd miss it.

They levered me into the back. She gave instructions to the driver, then got in beside me.

'Where are we going?'

'You'll see.'

'I don't want to go to a hospital.'

'Of course not.' She settled her shoulder bag into her lap. 'We're going to my flat.'

'Lisa is there? Your friend.'

'Lisa is not there.'

I subsided. We drove into the city again, but by a different route, which ran beneath the front of the Palace. Across the water the lights flicked gently, their reflections stirring. Grand Hotel, upside down. We drove for ten minutes, somewhere along the north side of Lake Mälaren, and when she got me out it was a ten-storey loop of modern flats with sculpture lurking on the lawn in front and a fountain playing in the lobby inside. The only light came from beneath the water. We crossed an expanse of parquetry to a bank of lifts, and were wafted up to the top.

Between them, Lisa and Eija were doing well for themselves. The wide living room had ceiling-to-floor windows across the full width, with no curtains. The light flowed up the other three walls and exhausted itself into the ceiling, so that I could see without reflections, from the chair in which she placed me delicately, that we overlooked the lake. Lights dotted it, and a pleasure cruiser drifted past like a string of gems tossed on the water. In a cabinet along one wall was Eija's modest collection of Sèvres.

She had gone straight into the bathroom. She came back, minus the little jacket, with a first-aid box in her arms.

'You haven't done anything to help,' she said severely.

'What would you suggest?'

'Your shirt off.'

'I'd like to wash my hands and face.'

She snapped her fingers. 'How stupid of me. I'm sorry, Owen. I'll get a basin.'

158

'I can make it.'

'I'll get a — '

'Eija, please, I have to go to the bathroom.'

Her chin puckered. I blinked and turned away. For a moment Karin had looked at me again. No more would happen when I amused her, than that Karin's chin would pucker. I'd always imagined that she'd been without humour, then she'd surprise me with that pucker.

Eija stood aside. She watched me gravely as I moved painfully across the floor, not assisting me because she realised the necessity of my independence.

I leaned over the elegant turquoise washbasin and stared at my face in the mirror. Two days of activity had trampled all over it. I washed my face, my back crying out when I dipped my head. In no way was I fit for heroics. Then I walked back to Eija, without my shirt, my hair tousled and my body already glowing with bruises.

'The return of the Viking,' she observed. 'Pillaged.'

I grinned at her, which in itself was painful. She sat me down in the chair. 'Now let me look at that forehead.'

She was close. I felt the perfume of her around my face. Her hands were delicate, drawing the pain from me.

'What did your wife say to you, Owen?' she asked casually. 'I didn't hear it clearly.'

'She told me not to head north.'

'That is good advice.'

'For a while I had the idea that she'd stolen my car, just to prevent me from going north. It would fit.' But only by stretching it to breaking point.

She touched the wound with something that made me flinch away. 'Baby,' she whispered. She had not commented on the theft of my car. 'There, that will do, I think. And I have something for the bruises. Lie on the bed, Owen.'

There was no bed in there. 'Can't you do it here?'

'If it pains you too much to —'

'I'm hurting all over.' Inside, too.

'I'll do it here.'

I watched her pouring something into her palm. 'But now I don't think it was Karin who stole my car,' I commented.

'Of course not.' She was brisk. 'She was in Hedemora, with *her* car. Where Anders Norgren was killed.'

She applied a palm to my chest, and moved it gently. Her lips were inches from my eyes, and her breasts moved provocatively beneath the blouse.

'I don't want to believe that,' I said.

'Of course you do not.'

This was said shortly, dismissing it, like a point already settled between us. I could sense the warm blood in her lips, and watch every millimetre of the scorn they lingered over.

'Of course you do not,' she repeated. She stood back to consider her progress with my poor body. 'That is because you are stubborn, Owen. You cannot bring yourself to accept that your Karin does not want you.'

I said nothing, because I was certain she did. Needed me, anyway.

She tossed her head in a small show of anger at my failure to agree. Then her voice softened. 'You are a fool with women, Owen. They can do anything with you.'

They? I supposed she'd included herself. I said gruffly, 'The way I see it, I've been getting clues to help me find her.'

She stood with cupped palm raised, the bottle in the other. In spite of her efforts a lock of hair fell over her eyes. She looked very appealing. She put down the bottle.

'Now lie back, Owen.'

I caught her wrist. Liquid spilled on the rug. 'No. This matters to me.'

'You're hurting.'

That stung like the liniment, and I released

her abruptly. She at once swept the lock of hair away with the back of her hand, and the rest of the liquid stained her blouse.

'The phone call was a clue,' I said, 'about the snow and the phone booth. That would mean Sweden to me, even how far I had to go north.'

She looked at me with Karin's own, unrevealing eyes. 'If you say so, Owen.'

'And the message on the back of the photograph,' I claimed.

'Which asked you to pursue it?' she asked scornfully. 'Pursue what?'

'I haven't sorted that out. Something to do with the picture, I suppose. But it was a clue, somehow or other.'

'You're so stubborn and . . . and contradictory.' I had to assume she meant contrary. She tossed her head. 'Will you please allow me to continue with this?'

I lay back. The liniment bit into me again. While I was still flinching, she said: 'But now she asks you *not* to go north.'

I drew in my breath. 'She mentioned north. A clue.'

'And I suppose she relied on the famous Owen Tanner stubbornness? She could assume you'd do the oposite to what she asked?'

'She understands me.'

162

'If she knew you . . . ' Slap, slap with her palms. ' . . . she would have known you could never understand the message in the photograph.' Rub, rub.

I reached up and stilled her hand. 'What's this about the photograph?'

She looked at me, I'd swear slyly. Then she offered, 'It was in her traditional dress.'

'What about it?' I whispered.

She shrugged and pouted, as though I'd dragged it from her, but we both knew she'd put it forward herself.

'These dresses are very regional, and confined to small areas. If she was born in Dalarna, say, the dress would locate her to a small portion of it.'

I sighed. 'But you didn't say anything about this.'

'I didn't want you to know,' she answered quietly, and her eyes were liquid.

'Protecting me?'

She nodded.

'From myself?'

'Your worst enemy, Owen my sweet.'

There was a flicker of humour in the corners of her mouth. Something that stood between us was crumbling away.

She laughed, and said: 'But now I can tell you, because you cannot go on with it, and it is all too dangerous and silly, and the police will know what to do.'

'But you reckon I'm safe here?'

'Lie back, Owen. I haven't finished this side.'

'What would I do without you?' I chided her.

'You must be serious.'

'Why must I? I am safe, I am happy here, soothed by your gentle hands . . . '

She was standing back. 'Now you are taking what you call the Michael.' She frowned. 'You must explain — '

'It means teasing.'

'Then you take me for a fool?'

'No,' I said gently. 'You're no fool, Eija. I'm the big fool around here. Led one way, pushed the other, manipulated and shoved around. I've just about had enough of it.'

'If you like to be stupid — '

'I like to be.'

'Such as trying to head north again?'

'I had that in mind, yes.'

She flung herself away from me. 'Oh, I have no patience with you. You could be in danger, Owen.'

'But from where? Nobody tries to kill me — '

'Then what is *that*?' she flared, pointing a finger at the plaster on my forehead. 'What is *that, that, that*,' coming in close and thumping her little fists against my individual bruises.

I shouted out in pain.

'And now I've hurt you,' she said angrily, as though it was my fault for feeling it. 'But what . . . ' She caught my hands, moving them up and down in rhythm with her urgency. 'What about tonight, in Gamla Stan?'

'All this damage is from Laurie's enthusiasm. The shot was meant to miss, a warning to stop me catching Karin.'

Now the tears were live in her eyes. 'I know . . . I *know* you are in danger. And I try so hard — '

By tensing my arm muscles I stilled the movement of my hands. I asked her softly, 'Was that why you stole my car and brought it to Stockholm?'

She searched my eyes, her chin puckering again, though not with humour, her lips quivering. Then she hammered my fists down onto my knees and flung her hands free in a wild flight of fury. 'Yes, yes! It was all I knew. All I could think — '

'Eija!'

Then she threw herself into my arms, sobbing into my ear, and I caught her tight, with pain shaking me and taking my breath. Just when I needed it.

'*Etkö sinä tajua, että minä rakastan sinua, senkin hölmö?*' she cried.

'English,' I gasped.

'I love you, Owen. I love you, and I want you to stop. Not go on. Oh . . . Owen!'

She was soft against me. Warm, sweet, loving Eija. I stood, bringing her up with me, and there was not one portion of me that was not soaked with her warmth. Her head was in the curve of my neck as I held her close, and suddenly this was another love that could be true or false, and I was so tired with the agony of indecision.

Eija's voice was murmuring softly. ' . . . poor, mixed-up Owen. Let me make up your mind — '

I groaned. She felt me stiffen in her arms, and withdrew her head, her eyes melting.

'What is it, Owen? Are you in much pain, darling?'

Across the room, on a plain pine table, the phone began buzzing, a repeated peep that I could have screamed at. She put a hand to the hair at my neck. 'Let it ring,' she sighed. But the spell was broken. I became aware again of the pain in my body.

'Better answer it.'

She turned away from me, glanced back darkly, then went to the phone. I couldn't hear what she said. Then she turned, holding

166

out the phone to me, her face stricken.

'It's for you.'

'But who — ' I stumbled, and righted myself.

As she handed it over she said one word as though in grief. 'Kent.' Then she turned her back on me.

'What the hell — ' I began.

'You met your wife tonight,' he said briskly. 'I want to know what she said to you.'

My wife! Karin was a stranger in that room.

'Owen . . . don't hang up.'

'She gave me advice.' I paused. 'Not to follow her north.'

His voice was astringent. 'We'll make sure you take it.'

'You can always try.'

Then I slammed down the phone. Eija was lighting a cigarette, the first I'd ever seen her smoke. The lighter was shaking.

'Damn him!' I shouted. 'Even here . . . he had to get at me, even here.'

'So little time,' she said softly, looking away from me and projecting her distress to the glowing sky outside.

'How did he know I'm here?'

She shrugged. 'He had somebody watching you, of course. One of Sjöberg's people. He reported back. It is simple.'

Her tone attracted my attention. My thoughts had been concentrated on my own distress, physical and mental, but now I saw she was quite as annoyed and upset as I was.

'I'm sorry,' I said. 'I've brought this into your life, and they're not going to leave us in peace, not for a minute. When I set foot in England again, then they'll relax. Here, they'll haunt me.'

'Here you could be safe,' she whispered.

But not safe from myself. They'd done their best to denigrate Karin in my eyes, soiling her, and she was part of me. I felt dirty, as though the dust of it had settled on my skin.

Eija touched my arm, and instinctively I drew away.

'Owen?' she whispered, with the hurt in her eyes.

To deny my own thoughts, I slid my arm round her shoulders. 'We could leave the phone off the cradle,' I suggested.

I wanted peace, just a little peace, for my mind to slow down and point me in a direction I would dare to take. I took her in my arms, unable to control a catch in my throat. She whispered to me, but there were no words I knew. Hope and joy fought to the surface and I caught her close, and now they were Eija's lips, Eija's hot, shining face between my palms and her smooth skin inflaming me.

'It's over,' she murmured. 'Finished, and gone.'

I groaned. She was urgent. Nothing was really gone; it simply stood aside.

The glow never really dies in the sky. Another day waits impatiently. We cried to each other, and the night opened out into a flash of dawn. In the pulse of our meeting she took my troubled mind and body to hers, and we melted into one ecstatic entity. We came together with the simplicity of mutual yearning. The urgency flowed through me, and we rushed to meet the light.

And then there was the soft setting of our sun, and the sky glowed gently again, green and purple, and in the other room the phone we'd forgotten was ringing.

There was nobody to answer it. We had gone away.

# 8

After a long while it stopped. Eija was asleep at my side, a warm, soft and pink cocoon. I lay on my back, smoking one of Eija's cigarettes. Women's cigarettes usually taste scented. Hers tasted of her lips.

It was strange how simple it was to think about Karin. I was standing — lying — outside and looking in, and from there I could see with intense clarity, when before, inside, there had been only swirling mists of confusion.

Niels Bergh now had the lot, the settings and the stones of the Tammela Necklace. He had needed Karin to lead him to the stones, and perhaps there was a personal attachment that I knew nothing about. He might also need her for future negotiations with the agents of the Finnish authorities. But for some reason that I couldn't understand, he also had need of me. I could hardly have cared less for his needs, but Karin's desperate plea for me not to go north had inferred a fear for me, and the fear could well include danger for herself. My objective was therefore simple. I had to meet her, face to face, and confirm the truth of this, and the extent of her own need. The extent of my own, too.

Then, perhaps, there'd be peace, and other possibilities to explore.

I slid from the bed. It was still night, but the glow was always there. I walked through to the other room, my legs stiff and aching, past the strewn discards of our clothes.

The phone sat silent, and from the great, wide window the shape of the opposite craggy shore was becoming visible. She called from behind me.

'Owen?'

'I'm here.'

'Come back to bed, darling.'

'I'm going to take a shower.'

She mumbled something contented. I showered and felt better. There was no razor, so the girls didn't trim their legs. It seemed a waste of time trying to fight off my beard.

She was in a light wrap, in the kitchenette, brewing coffee. I kissed the nape of her neck. She lifted her head and flashed me a smile.

'Lisa will not be back for a whole week. We'll move your things in here,' she decided.

I said nothing. I'd flung my slacks somewhere, and went to find them. She followed me, a mug swinging by its handle from one finger.

'I said we'd fetch your cases — '

'Please, Eija, you know what I've got to do.'

She believed I was cleansed, renewed and whole. I didn't like to tell her that I had to complete the treatment myself.

I had to be delicate, but I'm a fool with women.

'I thought we'd seen the end of that,' she said softly.

'Did you? But consider it.' I found my Y-fronts and struggled into them. 'Kent and the rest of them are chasing that Tammela thing. They've got no idea where to turn, but they know I'm the one with the clues. Do you really imagine they'll let me pack it in now, whatever they might say about keeping me out of it?'

'It's your life. You can do with it what you want to.'

I was impatient. That was a plausible fiction. 'Nobody can do what they want to. We're all in a web of our own surroundings, and of our own friends and enemies. Life's no more than a manipulation.'

'That's cynical,' she cried.

'It's how I feel. And I'm not going to rest — '

'Owen,' she shouted, 'stop it!'

I was very still, my belt half-notched. She came to me and hung her arms round my neck. The mug thumped between my shoulder blades. She whispered, 'You're such a fool, Owen. You let everybody use you. Manipulate, you said. It's a lovely word. You simply have to shrug them off.'

I searched her eyes. They were gentle. No deception. I was weakening, and had to resist it, so I said:

'It would be necessary, if Kent wanted to succeed, for him to get somebody close to me, Eija.' I chose each word with care.

She could have caught at the implication and withdrawn, before it wrecked both of us. But, smiling, she shook her head.

'You could stay with me. We can start to live.'

I was baffled. All sincerity swam in her dark eyes. 'But Eija, it was you who took my car.'

She frowned, perplexed. She had told me that, openly, and it had been for me.

'I thought at first it was Laurie and Cowboy,' I said. 'But my car's got an automatic transmission, and that means they'd have to short out the ignition *and* do something about the starter motor. That would take something of an expert, so I'd already decided it couldn't be them.' I listened to myself, drearily wondering whether it was me saying it. But I'd worked it out. Clever Owen.

'And then Cowboy told me the engine picked up at the bottom of the slope. It fired, and the car drove away. But you can't start an automatic car by running it down a slope. It doesn't turn the engine over.' She was watching every word being constructed by my cold lips.

'It had to mean it'd been started with a key,' I went on. 'You can't get round that.'

'I've told you it was me.' She was distant. Her eyes were clouded.

'You're missing the point, Eija. It was you, yes, but you'd have needed an ignition key. You could have come into the chalet when I was asleep. I'd left the door unlocked.'

'If I'd known that, I would have come to you.' The tiny echo of a fond smile.

I forced myself onwards. 'But you didn't use my keys, because they'd gone into one of my shoes, and you couldn't have found them.'

I'd gone on too long and elaborated too much. Her mouth was a line of pain.

'Eija?'

'You must go on. Do not let me stop you.'

I took a breath, and my ribs protested. I didn't want to believe it, but she'd offered no denial. 'Anders Norgren went north. He did that because of the clue about the snow under the edge of the phone booth. Kent told me that, but I hadn't said anything to Kent about the details of that phone call. I told it to you, Eija, and later I saw you speaking to Anders Norgren.'

She shook her head, lips tightly compressed. She withdrew her arms and stood back, the mug still on her finger. I was angry. She was standing there and allowing me to do this. She made no attempt to rescue me.

'And you have a way with the police, Eija. You speak to them and they go away. You smooth matters. And when it happened — when I was shot at — you were somewhere behind, talking to them again. Eija . . . you know what I'm asking. Tell me I've got it all wrong.'

She was having difficulty controlling her tears. 'You're not wrong.'

'You're with the police?'

'I'm an agent. Accredited was the word they used. A *free* agent. I can stop when I like.'

'And . . . the key?'

'You left it with your others in your front door, on the night your house was searched.

175

That . . . I was told. Your English police thought I might have . . . need to use a copy.' Her mouth twisted ruefully. 'It was not the use they had in mind, I'm sure.'

I fell into a pit. 'So now we head north together — is that the plan? Having pretended we could possibly stay here together, you're intending to let me have my way? And bloody well come with me! Not leaving my side for a minute!'

She threw the mug at the wall, and the smash shattered my anger.

'I didn't mean — ' I fumbled.

'They told me about you.' There were tears in her eyes, disgust in her voice. 'I had to know the person I was going to . . . meet, and they knew you when you were in the police yourself. Don't look at me like that! They were wrong, wrong. Is that my fault? Can I help it if you turned out to be . . . can I help it if I fell in love with you, damn you?'

'But Eija,' I stammered, 'when there was danger to me, when a man started shooting at me, you were a police agent again. You reported to them. For me, you did nothing. Nothing!' I said in appeal. 'Until later — here,' I added, remembering.

'I did nothing, then?'

She crossed the room in three angry strides

176

and swept her shoulder bag from where she'd thrown it. She fumbled inside, and produced something hard and blue.

'Nothing?' she demanded, leaning forward in her anger. 'I fired at him. With this!'

Then she threw it at my head. I put up my hand, more to protect my face than anything, caught it, and looked down at it. Why did it have to be a small automatic pistol, with its name inscribed on the side: Walther PPK — 6.35 mm?

I put it down on the small table, delicately, not to scratch the surface. I looked across at her. One word — the right word — would still have rescued it. I couldn't find that word. Or perhaps I didn't try hard enough. I heard myself saying, 'I'm going north.'

Her hand fluttered. 'My car — '

'I've got to go alone.'

I looked round. I had all I'd brought with me. No, perhaps less. But all I could carry. I stood by the door. 'Can't you understand, Eija?'

Then all I could feel proud about was that I managed to close the door without a sound. The thickest doors are the ones that close most quietly.

The lift deposited me gently in the vast foyer. The fountain played softly. I walked past it into the calm and balmy night, and

I began to walk. I didn't have to walk. I could have phoned for a taxi, because I'm very quick and bright and I already knew the Swedish for taxi. It's taxi. There — you see. Sharp. But I walked, because that was the mood of the moment, and the activity helped my muscles not to seize up, and because Eija knew me, only too well, and she would know I would walk, and she'd get out her car and follow me back to the sleeping city. Then, somehow, words would bridge the gap. And I'd have something to return to.

I put my head down and walked. I was a boy again, nine years old, and I'd left home, a rage at life carrying me out into the street, then the darkness and the vastness creeping into me with its fear at my heels, and the head down, walking, one foot plodding after the other, and still going when my father took my hand and said, 'A bit late to be out, young man.'

But this time nobody came to take my hand. The streets — and only ten minutes' drive from the city centre — were almost deserted. No car came from behind me. I stopped and looked back. There was nothing. Then I looked more carefully, remembering Kent's watcher, but I could not locate any unwanted shadows.

I walked. The night was clear and dry, and I realised it was cooler than I'd at first believed. I could have taken a taxi even then — I saw one cruising and could have hailed it — but I didn't know where I was heading. Not back to the hotel — it would have been a dead end of frustration.

The sun was close to rising when I plodded round the curve of street to the harbour. A few cars were moving about, a few people walking. I knew exactly where I was — five minutes from the Hotel Terminus. I turned away from it.

Round the sweep of the harbour the ships lay, the massed cluster of pleasure ships, the private yachts, the motor boats, the garden ships, the dilapidated hulks that might some day be repaired and drift out to sea. Hawsers creaked, with the occasional squeak and clink of the sprung tie-lines. I went slowly. The Grand Hotel slept with dimmed lights, the other side of the parking area. Across the water the Palace stood high as a dark bulk against the lighter sky. The sun touched the water with a bloody finger, and I hunted every corner, every shadow beneath the kiosks.

There was no sign of Laurie and Cowboy. A passing police car flashed a beam at me, and I stared into it angrily. They moved on.

I retraced my steps, and walked the other arm of the bay, over the Strömbron bridge to Gamla Stan. There was a curved fall of steps opposite the Palace, and several shapes were huddled there. But I'd have spotted the shape of Laurie's black box. These pitiful derelicts had nothing. At Slussen the huge statue of lovers was tinged with orange light, mocking me. Nothing. I turned away. A hundred yards across from the statue was the low wall where I'd sat, recovering, when Eija had found me. I started from that point, working uphill, and sideways in all directions.

The lifting sun could not penetrate into the confines of the Gamla Stan narrow streets. There were a thousand shadows to walk into and as many doorways to investigate. The window lights were dim — jewellers, art shops, engravers, silversmiths, artisans in all crafts. Not my two buskers, though. Not any buskers. My probing footsteps were loud in the night silence. A cat ran past me, and his spit of fear was a heart-jerking challenge.

The two white-gaitered guards outside the Palace gate watched me walk past them, only their eyes moving, their black automatic rifles tight across their chests. Laurie and Cowboy were not in Gamla Stan. I walked back down to the water, and the light was growing in the sky.

The possibility of finding them was very slight, I realised. I could search only where I'd already been, but they, too, had been in the same places. I headed for the Drottninggatan Steps, where I had first found them, taking the short cut through Kungsträdgården.

The birds were awake. The fountain still played, welcoming another day, and the geraniums were a glowing red in that light. I found them on a pair of benches, where the flower beds and bushes were laid back in arbours.

I stood looking at them, swaying slightly with weariness, and surprised that I should find such pleasure in uncovering these scruffbags. I was strung through with pain and my head was swimming. They sensed my presence. Laurie's bare head rose.

'Yeah, yeah,' he murmured. 'We move on.'

Then he saw it was me, and he was at once fully alert. His whisper cut the cool, moist air. 'Cowboy!' The fountain splashed behind me, as Cowboy blinked heavily awake.

They stared at me like hunted cats. I managed to grin at them.

'Some bodyguards you two are,' I said. 'Asleep on the job.'

'What's happened now?' Laurie demanded hoarsely.

181

'Nothing's happened.' When in fact everything had. 'You fellows said you wanted to head north. Am I right?'

Laurie nodded. Cowboy spoke with some enthusiasm. 'We sure do.'

'And so do I.'

They considered it. Laurie moved his feet with a gritty sound. Aquilegias framed his face dimly.

'When we've got a stake,' he said. 'There's good money here.'

'Not enough to find you a bed, though.'

'Saving it,' Cowboy told me.

'I'll stake you.' I nodded meaningly. 'My car's off the road. If I hire one the fuzz'll know, and I might just as well be on a string. So I need your help.'

They looked at each other. A cleaner in a white smock was doing an early round of the gardens. Cowboy nodded, but seemed nervous. Laurie rubbed his beard. I knew and they knew that I was asking Laurie to exercise his abilities in obtaining a vehicle for our use. The cleaner approached, rattling out empty cans from beneath the benches and dumping them in a trolley. I saw that it was a woman.

'Could be,' said Laurie at last.

I realised I'd seen his lips move. It was fully light, but barely four o'clock.

'When?' he asked. 'And where?'

'Outside the Hotel Terminus. That's on Vasagatan, opposite the railway station. Cowboy knows Vasagatan. It's where he sold the tripod.'

'Time, then, time?' said Laurie tensely. He'd got work to do on it.

'Shall we say . . . six?'

'You're pushin' it.'

'They're pushing me. Can you do it?'

'I can try,' he said, and Cowboy looked unhappy.

I remembered Laurie's hat, and threw it to him. 'You left that behind. You don't want your brain freezing up.'

He smiled, a twisted grin. 'Feels like it has. I reckoned you'd found it.'

I left them. By now I knew the way from there to the hotel. It was only a couple of minutes from the Drottninggatan Steps.

They had a man at the reception desk. I asked for my key, and as soon as I gave the room number he simply stood there, nodding beyond my shoulder.

The side of the foyer was set back into a wide alcove, with leather, studded chairs surrounding two long and low tables. The leather creaked as Dick Kent got to his feet. There was one single, low-powered wall-light, and the sun was hunting elsewhere. His hair was caught by the light, and the corners of his eyes gleamed. It made him look evil.

I stood, letting him come to me. 'I might have guessed.'

'Come and sit down, Owen. I don't intend to shout.'

I saw a chance of straightening out a point or two. I saw an opportunity of deceiving him, though not as to my general intentions. He knew very well I'd be making a move of some sort, but he didn't know when. I walked over to him, and he made a tentative gesture of friendship or sympathy, extending his hand. I didn't wish to touch him, and ignored it.

We sat, facing each other across a corner of the table. He had a glass of something, and I wondered how he'd managed to obtain it at that hour.

'You're late,' he said, almost as though he'd assumed I'd leave Eija's arms earlier.

'And you? Are you late or early?'

'I've been waiting for you. We've got things to discuss.'

Perhaps he was about to suggest we should go up to my room. I stalled that.

'Well . . . say what there is to say. I'm knackered.'

He looked down at the table, then took up his glass and sipped. I realised it was water.

He looked up and said:

'I've got reason to believe you're planning to head north, Owen.'

Had Eija informed them, to save me from heading into danger? She had a naive idea of the police mind. What did they care about any danger waiting for me? They wanted me to find Bergh for them, and they wouldn't be far behind.

'You've come to warn me off again?'

'I know you, Owen. You're forgetting that. You're awkward and unpredictable. You get these wild ideas of taking on the world. This is too big for you, mate. We don't want you messing it up.'

Was he sincere? 'You're not going to give me the chance, though, are you?'

He tapped the glass, gently but angrily, on the table. 'I don't understand what you're up to, and that's what's worrying me.'

'You're worried? Oh . . . I *am* sorry.'

'I'm warning you — '

'D'you think you ought to do that? Knowing my awkwardness, don't you think a warning might be a mistake?'

He looked beyond my head for a moment, then he sighed.

'I don't understand what it is between you and Karin, that's the trouble. But I can tell you she's poison for you, Owen. There's nothing there you'd want to face.'

'Isn't it marvellous . . . ' I leaned forward confidingly. 'Isn't it bloody wonderful how everybody knows how I should be thinking! Back off, Dick. Give me room for a thought or two of my own.'

He got to his feet abruptly. I looked at him, waiting.

'I can't talk to you.' His voice was tight. 'Don't try anything, that's all I'm saying.'

I nodded. He suddenly smiled. Now for the good news.

'Your car's ready.'

I stood, half stooped when my back caught me. 'They said two days. Maybe more.'

'We put some pressure on. We told them you had an urgent appointment in England.'

I stuck out my lower lip, petulant, like a child who's told to go to bed and knows he must.

'I'm *not* going home.'

He thought I'd run out of resistance. He spoke kindly.

'I'll send a man to run you out to Ulvsanda. Nine o'clock do you?'

I straightened wearily. 'Give me a bit of sleep, Dick. Say . . . nine-thirty?'

I went across to the desk and asked again for my key. When I turned with it in my hand, Kent had gone.

# 9

This time I took the larger, six-person lift up to my floor. I walked along the corridor to my door, opened it, and shut it with the gentleness of a man who has consideration for those still asleep. It nevertheless snapped, with a sound loud enough to be heard in the lobby. I was still standing on the soft carpet in the corridor.

I moved slowly back to the fire door. The lift still waited. I took the curving staircase that wound round the liftshaft, hand on the rail, padding softly. Then I could hear voices. I peered through the liftshaft tracery, round the final bend.

Sjöberg was talking to the receptionist. In the shadows by the steps down to the street door his athletic friend hovered.

I walked the last few steps, allowing myself to be heard, and trotted out to the reception desk.

'Did I leave a map . . . oh, it's you, Chief Inspector.'

'Good morning,' he said, beaming. 'Do you need a map?'

'I want to locate Ulvsanda, where my car is.'

'But surely Richard told you — I'm sending a car.'

'Yes. It's very good of you. But I'll need to check the route back here, to pick up my camera and cases.'

He clamped a hand on my shoulder. 'Nonsense. You can take it all out to Ulvsanda in the police car. Then they'll show you your best route from there.'

His was a face that inspired trust, a knobbly face that had clearly thrust itself into many an awkward situation. I smiled ruefully, a beaten and exhausted man.

'West?' I asked. 'Back to Göteborg?'

'Of course.'

We smiled at each other. It was all deception. He knew, as I did, that I was going to be heading north. All I could hope was that he didn't guess it would be so soon. I took the small lift back up to my floor.

My room was compact, and to the rear of the building. I opened the door again and went in, automatically reaching for the light switch, and suddenly surprised at the flood of sunlight that slanted in through the window. My clothes and my two suitcases were as I'd left them, my camera equipment untouched. I didn't reckon anything had been searched, but I was too tired to check. I put out a clean shirt and a change of slacks, and had the shave I'd missed at Eija's. God, it felt good. It was five o'clock, with no sense at all in trying for an hour's sleep.

I searched out the spool of sticky tape I carried in my holdall, and made an amateur repair of my pipe. It wasn't good, but it worked. Lighting it, I sat on the side of the bed, then took out the photograph again, just to make sure I hadn't misinterpreted the message on the back.

The writing was Karin's, and the moustache embellishment was clearly hers. It was not, perhaps — as I'd thought — a flash of her skittish sense of humour, but more likely a sign to me that it was really she who'd penned it. But why that should have mattered to her I couldn't imagine, as the words themselves were clearly Bergh's. Ballpoint, too. Now . . . that was unusual. She favoured a fountain pen.

*But you should pursue it.*

A curious phrase, like the advice from a headmaster to a schoolboy on his career.

And then, the sunlight being bright and almost horizontal, I thought I detected a run of fine dents on the surface. I moved the card, and they sprang up at me as words. It was as though the ballpoint pen had run dry on the final word.

Quickly, I hunted out a pencil, and shaded

across the surface. Eight more words became visible, white on black.

*Straight back home, Owen, if you love me.*

I sat very still, my heart thumping in my ears. The scene I had imagined in my room at the Hotel Gustav was now slightly changed. Niels Bergh in there with Karin — yes. The message had been dictated by him, as I'd guessed. The very contrast between the early words and the last ones was much like the original message over the phone. His words and hers. Now . . . his words: Clever darling. (What he would believe Karin would say). Then the unfeeling sentiment about the car. (Again, put in because he thought she should express concern.) But . . . sorry! Ye Gods! Sorry I left a body in. And the words: But you should pursue it. Ah, but those were his critically important sentiments. Once again there was his strange desire that I should continue to follow up the clues he left me.

For a moment my mind stalled on that point. Why should he need me? Then I shook my thoughts free, because the final sentence was for me, alone, and from Karin, personally and secretly.

Again there was the desperate plea for me to abandon the search. But she had added the words: if you love me. When a woman tells you to abandon her 'if you love me', you know damned well you'd better not do it. It told me she needed me, yet feared for my safety.

'Do not go north,' she had cried in the square at Gamla Stan. Combining both — the message enforced by Niels Bergh, with its clue, and again her personal plea.

I could see how she'd managed to leave me the secret message. It needed no more than a slip of paper between ballpoint and photograph, at a time when Niels took his eyes from her, perhaps to stare suspiciously out of the window. I could see, too, why it had to be in ballpoint. And yes . . . even the reason for the moustache. It was meant to tell me that there was something involving ballpoint for me to find.

She was travelling with him, but virtually controlled by him. There was danger. Hell, I knew that. Hadn't he shot at me when there was danger of my catching her? We were perhaps intended to meet, but it had been too soon.

Suddenly, everything had purpose. I wanted to charge out and challenge everybody — and where the hell were Cowboy and Laurie?

I packed my bags any old how, slung the holdall over my shoulder, clasped the tripod under the other arm, and headed for the lift.

I went down, and spread it all in front of the reception desk. I asked the man for my bill. He looked startled. I repeated the room number, and he told me my account had been taken care of. Leaving me no excuse for hanging around, no doubt. I snarled at him, and challenged him to touch one button on his phone console, whisper one word into his loop mouthpiece. He understood. He seemed nervous.

Six-ten, and they hadn't come. I went to the outer door and stood on the pavement. Cars were parked in front of the Central Station opposite, and on both sides of the street. Any one could have concealed a watcher. This was a one-way street. The direction was to my right, which was north, which was convenient.

Then I saw them. The car Laurie had obtained was a Saab of indefinite vintage, and was parked thirty yards away. They were both asleep in the front seats.

I went and hammered on the windscreen, and they came alive like curled hedgehogs from hibernation. I ran back for my bags. The receptionist was gabbling into the phone, so I threw a kroner at him. 'For the call.' Then Cowboy was there, helping me. I thrust the tripod into his hands.

'You might need it again.'

'Aw . . . come on.'

They bundled me into the back. The box, their haversack, and the guitar gave me very little room, when all of me and mine were inside. Then Laurie took off with a roar of split silencer and a scream of bald tyres.

'This is north!' he shouted. 'Great!'

'Turn left as soon as you can,' I told him.

'You said — '

'They'll be after us in no time. You've got to shake 'em loose.'

'Leave it to me.' Laurie half-turned his head. His teeth flashed.

'No. Head west. Let 'em think I'm going home.'

He shrugged. Cowboy was gripping the fascia, and we swooped up an incline to an island.

'Left here!' I shouted, and he took me literally, left on the wrong side of the road, and circling the island the wrong way. An early bus howled at us, and we shot from under his nose.

'Soon drop 'em,' cried Laurie confidently.

He might have been marvellous on a stolen motorcycle. In a car, he was agony. He seemed to think he could lean it into corners. I groaned, visualising our escape being curtailed with abrupt embarrassment.

'Get on the E3,' I pleaded. 'Give yourself some room, Laurie.'

And myself time to think.

My memory of the map was that there was a road bridge across the easterly end of the lake, and the next one across it was as far away as Strängnäs, sixty or so miles. Any intention of travelling north seemed to indicate that the lake should be kept to our south.

After a great deal of rocking round corners and hooted protests from other motorists, I spotted a junction sign ahead — E3. North to our right, south to our left. I had to make a snap decision, and north was too obvious.

'Turn left,' I shouted.

Laurie did it. He'd got used to going the wrong way round junctions, and we survived. Then we plunged over water, which had to be Lake Mäleran, and my die had been solidly cast.

I was turning from time to time, looking for followers.

Strangely, no police car was scything the landscape with its siren. I was suspicious. But now, on the motorway, the traffic was thinning out. It gave me a chance to observe, and after we'd by-passed Sodertälje I located him. A blue car, the same blue that I'd spotted in Hedemora, but at that time a woman had been driving it. A blond woman, I'd thought. This time the driver was alone, and it seemed to be a man. It was rather obvious that it had to be Niels Bergh, checking that I was following his clues.

'There he is,' I said. 'A blue Citroen. Can't you go any faster, Laurie?'

'Foot's through the floorboards already.'

The blue car was holding us without effort. There was no possibility that Laurie and I could change places, which was a pity. I knew a few tricks he didn't.

'How are you on country roads?' I asked.

'Heh . . . them snakey corners!'

I shuddered. 'Try it. Look for a turn-off, and head for the hills.'

It was a figure of speech. I saw no indication of hills on either side. But Laurie took the next turn-off with enthusiasm. We did a large circle, plunged under the motorway, and came out heading south. We were now doing exactly the opposite to what I'd wanted.

'Country roads!' said Laurie in disgust. 'We're comin' up to a soddin' town.'

It wasn't much of a town, one set of traffic lights and four hundred yards of nerve-stretching early traffic. Laurie put his hand on the horn. I saw him do that, hard down on the horn ring. But no sound came out. We emerged onto a country road, winding, climbing gradually through pastureland.

We had found our hills, but now I couldn't think what to do with them. The Saab began to labour. This didn't really matter, because our follower wasn't interested in catching up with us. But the ease with which he was maintaining station hardly encouraged me to suppose we could shake him on the downhill stretches. If we ever came to any. We were climbing, climbing. Trees edged us closely and the sun was a forgotten luxury, up there amongst the tracery. The road became narrow, wound more, and twice we thumped across bridges, beneath which swept rushing mountain streams. There was a shallow ditch on each side of the road, and then trees, trees. We met no other vehicles. The pines reached high for the light, the bark brown or stripped by the winter.

'He still with us?' asked Laurie.

'What d'you think! Haven't you got a mirror?'

'Cowboy bashed it in with his forehead.'

'Come on,' I said. 'Drive, damn it.'

Then I wondered why we had to drop the car. I tried to think of a good reason, but every time a thought started to crystallise, Laurie's driving jerked it free.

We were skirting a mountain, running round it. Far below, water winked. The trees clad the hillside like a grey-green carpet, and between them, below us, we could see the road, writhing in loops and whorls. We began the descent.

'I'll drop him now,' said Laurie complacently. The speedo needle crept up, and the only change was that we snaked in and out of the bends with wilder abandon, and the blue car sat firmly on our tail, gracefully sweeping where Laurie had scrambled before.

'He's still there,' I commented, having decided I didn't care, anyway.

'All *right*,' he shouted. 'I'll get him.'

I could see his intention before he put it into effect. Dive at a sharp corner, lurch round it, and come to a skidding halt, side on. I shouted to him not to try it. Confrontations I did not want.

He snarled 'I'll get the bleeder.'

I wondered if he hoped to crash him.

Then we were into the corner. He took it too fast and too close. His front wheels locked, and we spun twice, then came to a shuddering halt. The nearside wheels went down with a thump. It had the intended effect — it blocked the road. But it left me so shaken that I could barely drag myself upright, and Cowboy's head had had another go at the rear-view mirror.

The Citroen came round the bend, sighing into the camber. The trees had completely screened us, but he did well. When he came to a halt he hadn't scratched his finish and hadn't spun. But his off-side wheels were in the left-hand shallow ditch, spraying gravel and dust in a shower. The car was creeping forward.

Laurie fell out of the Saab on hands and knees, scrambled up, and ran across the road. He slammed his palm on the top of the roof, jerked open the passenger's door, and shouted angrily:

'What's the game, mister?'

I managed to get my door open and my feet onto the ground. Cowboy was standing outside the car and reaching with his big hand, I thought to help me. He put it on my chest and thrust me back again.

'You keep outa this.' There was something in his eyes that I hadn't seen before, a cold determination, a stir of anger. He'd been infected by Laurie's fury. A trickle of blood ran from a cut on his forehead. He turned, and ran across to join Laurie.

'Get outa there,' Laurie was demanding. 'Let's have a look at y'.'

I climbed out of the Saab. Nothing was happening how I wanted it. The scene was falling apart. I walked up behind Laurie and Cowboy, and the driver had said nothing.

Then he decided to come out and discuss it. He slid his legs over the gearbox console, then his body, and he was out on the road and straightening. The whole movement had been completed with smooth and unhurried grace. His hair was close-cropped. He had a soft and insignificant chin and his nose was long. I had last seen him in Hedemora. His face was impassive, his eyes expressing nothing. His passivity stirred an uneasiness in me.

'What's with the following, mate?' Laurie demanded. He'd moderated his voice. Perhaps he'd noticed the eyes. 'You got any right to tail people?'

Cowboy was at Laurie's shoulder. He could sense that Laurie was losing control of the situation, and moved up beside him.

'Let me take care of this,' I said. If anybody could. The eyes were deadly.

But Cowboy was well into his act of bodyguard. He stepped forward. The driver was clearly not overjoyed with the situation. A confrontation was not his idea, either. This was the man who had murdered Anders Norgren. I felt cold and empty.

He looked into Cowboy's eyes. 'Get from underfoot, chicken-shit,' he said softly.

Then he made a move to climb back into the car. Cowboy's hand reached out and clamped on his shoulder, and Bergh stopped, very still, head ducked to slide into the Citroen. He looked round. I could see his teeth. He hissed like my bun-seeking swan, then, so fast I couldn't see where it had started from, the edge of his hand chopped down on Cowboy's wrist.

Cowboy grunted. His hand fell away, and he grabbed his shoulder, where the pain would terminate.

'By God,' shouted Laurie, 'you'd better — '

But Cowboy threw him aside with his good hand advanced, his first now a clump of bone and flesh. He moved fast. Bergh had not straightened from his crouch. His other hand was still inside the car. Then he brought it out, and I just caught the dark blur as the pistol came with it. The two shots were so close together that they sounded as one, and the echoes rocked away amongst the trees. He looked across at me once, briefly, his teeth bared, then he plunged back inside the car. He was behind the wheel before Cowboy began to buckle at the knees.

'Ron!' screamed Laurie.

It was the first time I'd heard Cowboy's real name. I watched gravel fly as the engine roared. The Citroen lifted with a sigh and flung itself from the ditch, snaking with howling tyres as it searched for grip. Then it was away.

'Ron, you gotta — '

Cowboy had rolled as he fell, and his face was looking up at me. I could have told Laurie that Cowboy hadn't got to do anything any more, and there was no use in pulling and tearing at him, and slapping his face in fury at the lack of response. I could have told him Cowboy was already dead.

Laurie was on his knees, pounding at his brother's chest. 'Come on! Come on!' he cried.

I had never felt so helpless. Fifteen years in the force, and I didn't know what to do. It was as though the impact of the bullets had reached out to me, and the sheer vicious finality of it drew every spot of blood from my brain.

'Laurie,' I heard myself saying. 'It's no good. You can't — '

And then I stopped. There was nothing worth saying, in the face of Laurie's grief. He was completely bereft, sobbing now. Desperately I looked round for help. I must have subconsciously sensed or heard something. A car was drifting round the corner, and I could see it was Eija at the wheel. She coasted it to a halt, then she sat where she was, staring at me through the windscreen. Staring . . . staring . . .

For a moment I'd taken my eyes off Laurie. When I looked back he was running towards the Saab. I shouted, but he couldn't have heard. He was locked in his own personal conflict.

'I'll get the sod. I'll get him for y' . . . ' he was shouting back to Cowboy.

He had the car moving, working dementedly at the wheel. I ran in front of it, but he didn't see me, and I had to jump clear. His face was old.

Then he was gone in a scramble of missed gears, and I watched as he took the next corner, with one rear wheel lifting. He hadn't hope of catching the Citroen.

Eija was standing over Cowboy. She crouched down beside him and tried his pulse, then the artery in his neck. She got to her feet. She didn't have to say anything.

'That was Niels Bergh in the Citroen,' I said.

'I know.' She was not looking at me now. There were dark shadows under her eyes, and her mouth was set in an uncompromising line. She was painfully formal.

'We shall have to follow him,' she said. 'We should try not to lose him.'

'But you can't leave Cowboy here,' I protested.

'I don't think he'll mind.' She was cold and distant.

In anger, I burst out, 'Not lying here, like a pile of rubbish — '

Then at least she did look at me, and I flinched from the contempt in her voice. 'And now, I suppose, you can blame yourself for this!' She gave a small grimace, despising herself for having said it. 'I'll get help, then we'll have to go.'

I went with her to her car. We sat inside, and she snapped open the cover of the glove compartment her side. It had been enlarged, and inside it was a police R/T set. She took up the mike and spoke crisply for a minute in Swedish. She tucked it all away, then she turned to me. It had all been very efficient.

'Somebody will be here in five minutes. Is that all right?'

I was searching for words. What could I say to her?

'Is that arrangement satisfactory?' she asked, not making a move until I was happy with it.

'Drive,' I told her, 'if you have to.'

She started the engine and let in the clutch, and we slid off in pursuit. It was not the car she'd told me was hired, but a

203

smart, tight little Alfa Romeo, and I realised that it was probably her own, certainly not another hire car, with that R/T set they'd put in it. She was driving as though she knew the car well, positioning the nose for each hairpin, accelerating out with barely a waver from her chosen line. We were moving fast, the road looping down the hillside. I realised that now the lower slope was less obscured by trees. The foresters had stripped it, and huge piles of stacked pine logs were waiting, white-grey ghosts, lining the road at intervals. From time to time I thought I saw the movement of a vehicle farther down towards the glimpses of water.

The road surface deteriorated abruptly. In Sweden they seem to strip the whole width of their minor roads when they're resurfacing. We thudded and bumped through a mile of potholes and rocks, the smaller stuff rattling on the undersurface. She juggled for the best line through it, our speed right down to what seemed a crawl.

'Why only you?' I said.

'I do not understand.'

'Only you on our tail — or rather, on his.'

'They expected you to wait for your car.'

'But not you?'

'I know you, Owen, only too well.'

But with two murders, now, the whole country should be on the alert. I said that. She didn't glance at me.

'They will be.' She nodded. 'But it is probably easier to follow you. In the end, you will find him for us.'

'And find your precious necklace?' I said in disgust.

We reached metalled surface again, and the speed rose. She flashed me a sudden, brittle smile.

'Or your precious Karin.'

She took a left-hander that left me hanging over space for a second, but I hardly noticed it. Suddenly, rage had flooded me, a reaction I suppose. Two murders for a handful of stones and a bloody setting! National heritage, my arse. Most of every country's national heritage consists of loot taken by force, with bloodshed and death and dishonour framing it. Yet now it is all treasured, the blood having been washed from it by time. But this necklace would be spattered with fresh blood.

My precious Karin, she called her. They'd done their best with her image, but I still preferred the tarnished Karin to any amount of sapphires and emeralds and rubies, however much they polished them and however well they were reset.

I nearly burst out with it. Very nearly told Eija about Karin's private message to me. But it remained my secret.

'You don't know about Karin,' was all I said.

'And there're still things *you* don't know about her.'

I was about to demand angrily what they were, but she cut me short.

'Look. Ahead there.'

We had swept round a right-hander that seemed to go on for ever. Below and in front of us the road suddenly became steeper, and snaked before it reached the next hairpin. Tucked into the rockfall against the steep hillside was the Saab. As we ran down to it I could see steam rising from the radiator.

We drew in behind it, and I ran forward. There was nobody inside. Eija called to me:

'He's there.'

She was standing on the outer edge of the road, looking downwards. I ran to join her. Two loops were visible, on the second a miniature blue car moving, it seemed, slowly. Laurie was halfway down the first portion of the slope, leaping the pine stubs, which now seemed far apart without their lofty heads, pounding down headlong with his arms flying for balance. He was aiming to head off the car. I couldn't see what he could do if he did; his rage and distress wouldn't stop it.

'He'll never do it,' I shouted.

But then I saw that he was waving in his right hand something that could well swing the odds.

I galloped back to the Saab. On the front seat Laurie's black box was open. He had lifted out the recessed top shelf, scattering the stripped-down sax and clarinet on the floor. It left a space below, two inches deep. But it was empty now, apart from the three steel clips fastened to the base.

I turned. Eija was standing very still at the road edge, shielding her eyes. The sun was high, now, and a blue mist blurred the distant trees.

'He's got a gun!' I called.

'I can see that.'

She turned to me. The sun slanted across her face, casting a shadow from her flying hair like a whiplash across her cheek. Her eyes were very bright, accentuated by the dull shadows beneath.

'Owen — your friend has a gun.' She pointed the responsibility at me.

'I didn't know!' I protested.

I turned back to the car, a sudden thought catching my breath. I hauled out the guitar case, tore the instrument from it, and flung it down on the grass verge. Savagely I drove my foot through it, with a sick feeling as though I was crushing Cowboy's coffin. But he'd only had four chords! Strapped with adhesive tape to the back panel was a .38 Smith & Wesson automatic pistol.

It was Cowboy's fall-back weapon, for use in emergency. But what emergency had he anticipated that would necessitate the smashing of his own guitar?

Eija reached past me and unpeeled the tape. 'I'll take that, I think.'

'No, I'll — '

But I didn't know what I was saying. She expertly slid out the magazine. It was fully-loaded. She worked the slide, and there'd been one in the breech.

'Come away, Owen.'

Nothing, just nothing that I touched was as it seemed. There was no desire to move from there, and have to face any more misconceptions.

'You must come away,' she said softly, and I turned to face her.

The tension had eased from her face. Her lips were moist, her eyes full of the compassion of a mother watching a hurt child. I didn't want her pity. I waited until she turned away, then I stumbled after her to her car.

# 10

We came down out of the snake of mountain roads, and we did not see Laurie below us. There were now other vehicles on the roads. We crept a full mile behind a tractor with a wide tow of farm machinery, and it was from there that I turned to look back up the slope.

'There,' I said. 'There he is.'

We stopped and got out. He was a tiny, dark figure, clambering straight up, the way he'd come down. He was still one slope short of where he had started. We got back into the car, and caught up with the tractor in two minutes.

'We might as well turn back,' I said, my mind beginning to function.

She drove on.

'I've left all my stuff in that car,' I said, my voice more firm. The anger was still with me, but it was cold, in storage.

'If Niels Bergh is heading north, then he can cross at Strängnäs, or he might head all the way round the lake at Kviksand. We could still intercept.'

'Nonsense. You radioed the information — the

209

police will do the intercepting.' If that was what they wanted.

She glanced at me. The tractor turned through a gateway, and she drew to a halt beyond it.

'I thought you'd like to hear he's been caught,' she offered.

I shook my head. 'I just want to reach Karin.'

She backed into the opening the tractor had used, and swung out from it. Then she retraced our route.

'But now you're in difficulties, aren't you, Owen?' she said.

'You've got no alternative but to trust me, because your own car's back in Stockholm, and you're here with me. All right, so I'll take you north — we'll go to Dalarna. I'll do that even though you know I don't want you to go there. And even though you know I'm working with the police.' There was a pause. 'Owen?'

Her voice had been rising. I'd made only a muttered protest, no specific words, but it seemed to bring it to a head. All she'd have needed was a movement of my little finger. She'd contained it long enough.

'You've got to trust me,' she burst out, 'because I daren't let you out of my sight.'

Then the car lurched to a halt as she

210

braked violently. She sat in the stationary car and beat her fists on the steering wheel.

'But if you look at me once more, Owen, as though I am some sort of enemy . . . ' She drew in her breath. 'I am *not* your Karin. I do not intend to lead you or bully you or encourage you — or whatever she did with you. I am me. And if you stare at me with that expression again, I swear I'll throw you out of this car, and let you *walk* to Dalarna, if you wear your legs to the knees. I am not Karin, . . . I am me!' She stopped, sobbing. At last she choked, 'Just let me account for my own faults, Owen.'

'Yes,' I said, numb and miserable with her pain.

'What the hell's that?' she shouted. 'Yes! Yes!'

Karin would never have cried out to me with passion; it was I who had depended on her.

'Yes,' I said, clearing my throat. 'I'll remember all that. But it's Karin we're going to.'

She nodded. She reached and produced a handkerchief and dabbed her eyes. 'As long as you realise it's me who's taking you.'

Then she drove back to the crashed car. Her profile was stiff and formal with pride, but it was her own pride, and she was quietly satisfied with it.

There was a police car standing by the Saab, with two officers, a man and a woman, talking to a young man in motorcycling kit and no crash helmet. We parked and went across, and Eija spoke rapidly in Swedish. Then she turned to me and gave me a summary.

Laurie had been waiting there by the car, and had waved down this young man, who'd leaned his bike onto its propstand, removed his helmet, and walked forward to see if he could help. Then, with one quick blow to the side of his jaw, Laurie had knocked him out. When he came round Laurie was walking from the car, crash helmet on his head but unstrapped, with his kit-bag over his shoulder. With not one glance at his benefactor, Laurie had straddled the bike, dumped the kitbag across the tank, and ridden away, back in the general direction of Stockholm.

He had probably passed the patrol car, but they hadn't been looking for a motorcyclist. He would also have passed the dead body of his brother, but the ambulance would have been there.

I went to look in the car. Laurie, I'd gathered, had another Honda, a fast 750 cc four-cylinder job. He also, I saw, had his sax and clarinet with him, though he'd left the black box. It had most likely proved too bulky for the bike. He'd not touched my holdall. The Canon A-1 and my flash equipment, the lenses, the spare films, they were all intact. My cases were still there and unopened.

But my tripod wasn't anywhere I could see it. I searched, inside and outside, but there was no sign of it. I turned to Eija, baffled and uncomfortable with the thought.

'He's taken my tripod.'

She was studying my face. 'Why are you looking like that? What is it?'

'I don't know what it is,' I said impatiently. 'But something stinks to high heaven.'

'Stinks?' She wrinkled her nose. A word she didn't know, but could smell.

'It worries me. Can we get moving?' I asked.

'Bring your other case,' she said, taking hold of one of them. 'North?' she asked, as though there was any choice.

'As fast as you can.'

Perhaps I shouldn't have put it like that. My nerves weren't good, anyway, and she did nothing to soothe them. She drove with silent concentration, and I decided not to disturb it. I sat back. I gave some serious thought to what had happened.

It was clear that Laurie and Cowboy were no more buskers than Eija was the Countess of Tammela — if they had countesses in Finland. I had to accept that they were crooks, who intended — or had already started — to conduct an armed foray on the unsuspecting Swedes. From that starting point, it was easy to see that they weren't as short of money as they'd pretended, the busking being a neat cover, when I came to consider it. Then why did Cowboy sell my tripod? Could he really have been that subtle? But the end had justified the means, because it had confirmed my impression that they were quite impecunious, and at the same time it had made certain that I would search them out in Stockholm.

The more I thought about it, the more I liked it — or appreciated it, anyway. As buskers, they could be reasonably certain I'd be able to search them out with a good chance of success. And I? Well, I was part of their scene. I was the big goon who ran them from place to place so conveniently. I was their background cover.

Oh, but I'd fallen for it. I always fell for everything, I thought sourly.

But I couldn't work out why Laurie had now taken my tripod, unless he thought it still maintained his cover as a busker. He wouldn't know I'd seen the pistol in his hand; might not have noticed I'd found Cowboy's. I was not pleased with it, but Laurie's confused mind, still in shock, might have seized on anything that linked with his busking.

I wondered what sort of tune he played with a handgun.

The tyres thrummed over a level crossing, and we turned left.

'We're entering Strängnäs now,' Eija said.

We came down into the town. In the bright midday sun it seemed more like a holiday resort. The U of the harbour was packed with pleasure vessels, motor boats, yachts, and rowing boats. Colours crackled and the water sparked with sun. Children ran and screamed, and stalwart, bronzed Swedes were mucking about in their boats.

Eija glanced at me. 'There should be a bridge.'

I couldn't see a bridge. According to the map the lake narrowed there, and Strängnäs straddled a long finger of harbour. But there should have been a bridge. She slowed the car and called out to a passer-by:

'*Kan du tala om var bron är?*'

There was a flow of dialogue and pointing fingers. Eija let in the clutch. '*Tack,*' she

215

cried. 'We drive round the bay,' she told me.

The road hugged the line of the water. A yacht was drifting out, flapping canvas reaching for the breeze. On our right, on a slope above us, a red windmill stood with its sail motionless. Once around the corner we saw the bridge. There was a sharp, rising left-hander to get onto the roadway.

They had set up a roadblock the other side of it. Eija got out and went to speak with a bearded sergeant. I saw her show him an identity card. They spoke together for a few moments, and she came back.

'They have not seen a blue Citroen.'

'And the bike?'

'There are too many Hondas.' She shrugged. 'Too many possibilities.'

We drove on. After a while we stopped to top up the tank and eat a quick meal.

'Want me to take the wheel?' I asked, just itching to try the Alfa. 'It'll give you a rest.' And calm my nerves. She took corners as though they fed themselves beneath the wheels, but there was always the chance that one of them wouldn't know the trick.

She shook her head. 'You'd drive too fast.'

'We might have to hunt around, and there's no point in taking it so easy.'

She had no ear for sarcasm. 'But think of it, Owen. There is no real hurry.' So perhaps she had.

My coffee was too hot. I put the cup down again. My nerves were tattered with urgency. 'I don't understand. Why isn't there any hurry?'

'You're in the middle of it, and you don't understand? Everything's revolving around you. That should be clear to you now. Nothing can happen until you get there.'

I sipped. It was still too hot.

'Get where, for heaven's sake?'

'Where she wants you to go. She's leading you on a string, Owen.'

I looked at her suspiciously, but her nose was crinkling and her eyes were mischievous. I grunted, unsure how to react now that I knew the leading came from Niels Bergh.

'Such a remarkable woman,' she said, 'who can persuade Owen Tanner to go in *any* direction. Except his own.' She got up from the table. 'Come along — haven't you finished your coffee yet?'

I trailed after her, laughing because she expected it, but nevertheless she did drive more slowly, as I sat with the map on my lap and called out the towns ahead.

'Enköping. Sala. Avesta. Hedemora.'

'Hedemora?' I repeated.

'Is it surprising? We're moving into her home territory.'

But I stared ahead at the unreeling road. Hedemora! *Straight back home, Owen, if you love me.* But I was not doing so. In . . . I checked on a signpost . . . in thirty-two kilometres' time we'd be heading through Hedemora, and in no way was I going straight back home. I felt relaxed, but poised. Karin had known she could depend on me.

Then we were through it, or rather, had skirted it, and it seemed that I was the right side of a barrier.

'And it's not surprising,' Eija was saying, 'that she managed to get to Sweden with the stones. I'm talking about your wife, Owen. Please pay attention, it's something else you should know about her. The police were not alerted until nine in the morning, when they discovered Gunnar Bergh's body in the strongroom.'

I made the mental adjustment, back to England and back in time. She must have been saying something that I'd missed.

'You're saying she headed straight for Felixstowe and got on the ferry?' I asked. The image thus evoked was unpleasant. Scuttling for safety, and leaving the two men . . .

But Eija was speaking softly, the engine hum now restrained.

'It was a Sunday. The two men opened the strongroom door about midnight. Hammerstein, the owner, who'd been commissioned to do the resetting and polishing, was at his weekend retreat in North Yorkshire, at Whitby. At about four in the morning Hammerstein's housekeeper was roused by a frantic woman wanting to speak to him. All the housekeeper could say was that he'd gone to Whitley Bay, to take a trip on a friend's yacht from there. That would have been about two hundred and fifty miles from London to Whitby, then another sixty or seventy to Whitley Bay. At a little after five, a woman was seen by a policeman walking up and down the front at Whitley Bay. She said her husband had gone out fishing, and hadn't come back, and he assured her that people did fish all night. But she went on pacing.'

'You know this well.'

'I have read the reports.'

'You know my country well.'

She pursed her lips. 'I studied the maps. It hadn't seemed possible.' She glanced at me, but I had no more to say. She went on, 'At nine o'clock she was still there. A café proprietor saw her when he opened up. At nine-thirty the phone rang in Hammerstein's office. A police sergeant answered it. He asked who it was, and a woman simply said, 'Is he alive?' He asked her to give her name. The man was a fool. She asked again if he was alive, and he replied, if she meant the man in the strongroom, no. She hung up.'

I took a deep breath.

'She was only a few miles from Newcastle docks,' said Eija. 'They did not even know about her for three days, so that was how they came to miss her. And it was another week before they found the car she'd stolen, in the car park at the docks.'

I turned in my seat. She was smiling very gently, sadly. She realised I was watching her.

'I said, didn't I, Owen? A remarkable woman, your wife.' There was not the faintest trace of cynicism or bitterness in her voice.

Around the age of sixteen I'd realised I didn't understand women. Since then I've wasted a lot of years trying to.

'You didn't have to tell me this,' I said.

'But I *did*.'

'Why? Why, in heaven's name?'

'For the same reason that I'm driving you north. There's got to be an end to it, a clean

220

break, one way or the other. Is it Falun after Borlänge?'

'No. I think we want Leksand.' I stared at the map, my eyes not really seeing it.

Eija was driving with a relaxed confidence. Suddenly I was afraid. Two inflexible women, and I was in the middle.

The map came into focus as she asked sharply: 'Are you sure?'

Yes, I was sure. There, on the map, was the spread of blue of another large lake. Lake Siljan. I remembered then the lettering on the two pieces from Karin's yellow vase. She'd spoken often of the lake, but never, as far as I could recall, mentioned its name. 'Sil — ' it had said on one piece of the base. ' — mics' it had said on the other. Siljan something!

'Yes, I'm dead certain,' I said.

Memories were swamping me. What she'd said of her childhood home, of the lakeside chalet they'd used for holidays when she'd lived in Stockholm. 'You could see the church from the chalet,' at one time. At another: 'On the first Sunday after midsummer, I went to church in that dress, Owen.' That was the dress in the photograph. Another comment I recalled was: 'I was standing with my back to Karl Kock — ' I snapped mental fingers in annoyance, but couldn't get his surname.

No, it'd been Kock Karl something. A friend, probably. ' . . . and I could see the chalet,' she'd said, 'through the star in the cross.'

My voice was unsteady. 'We've found the lake. Leksand is at the southern end of it. Yes, I'm sure we want Leksand.'

'Borlänge is right ahead. Then it's Leksand.'

I was tense, now, and excited, as if I were coming home after a long absence. We stopped for a cup of coffee at Borlänge, but I was eager to get on.

We came into Leksand from the south, sweeping right onto the bridge, over what looked like a river with no current. The lake — this narrow part of it — opened out on my left. I was twisting in my seat, eager to miss nothing. Eija turned left as we drove off the bridge, and pulled into a limited-stay parking place, nose in to the pavement.

'Why've you stopped here?'

'You should use your eyes, Owen.' She gestured. We were outside a Turistbyrǹ. 'They know everything at these places.'

I went with her to the door, but remained in the doorway, standing in the sun, restless, and with my eyes darting. Karin could walk out of a shop at any moment, or she could turn a corner. And she could walk away from me!

But there were too many slim and sleekly-tanned Swedish blondes, striding in linen trousers that ended below the knee, their bosoms moving gently in their bathing-suit tops. Eija came to my side. The tourist bureau had given her a blue leaflet with the title: Siljan Runt. A circular tour of the lake.

'There are hotels at a village called Tällberg. It is twelve kilometres along the lakeside road.'

'Tällberg?' I said.

'And there we must look for Siljansgřden, where there is a young woman who is an authority on traditional folk costume. You can show her your photograph . . . Why are you looking like that?'

I must have been grinning insanely. 'When you mentioned the railway junction at Hallsberg, there was something familiar in the name. But now I remember. Karin mentioned Tällberg, I'm sure.'

'Your memory,' she said severely, 'is erotic.'

'Eratic. But that too.'

'And the letter 'A' is pronounced differently. It has two dots over it.'

'Shall we get moving?'

'But really, Owen, you should try to get it right.'

'Are you *coming?*'

She smiled. My sense of humour was going sour. We drove back to the bridge, and turned left before we crossed it.

We were soon out of Leksand, and once again we were in the trees. But the pines, here, were in some way different, not so tall, not so impenetrable. I realised that we were probably quite high above sea level. The sunlight fell in a speckled mat on the tarmac, and the road wound tantalisingly, so that with every turn I expected to see something I'd recognise. A caravan site slid past on the left, with the sparkle of the lake beyond it. Karin had not mentioned it, but perhaps it'd not been there in her time.

A sign on the grass verge said: Tällberg, and then, as we swept round another bend, the green and white fingerboards began to invite us in profusion. Dalecarlia Hotel. Green Hotel. Tällbergsgården. Långbersgården Hotel. And: Skilift. This was a holiday area, probably mainly winter sports. But I began to worry whether we would find accommodation here, in spite of the choice of hotels. It was the middle of the summer, after all.

I snapped out of it, shouting: 'Stop! Hold it!'

She pulled to a halt. 'Owen?'

I pointed. The wooden-fronted shop was set back from the road, and had its own small car park. Across the front, above the wide window, was the sign:

## SILJAN KERAMICS

The yellow vase!

She parked beside the building, and we went inside. Tables and roof-high shelves were loaded with a hundred different designs of dishes, bowls, vases. In a far corner a woman was sitting at a bench, the paintbrush in her fingers flowing around the naked, baked-clay surface of a lamp base.

'*Goddag*,' she said.

I asked her if she spoke English. She completed a beautiful curve, then came to the counter. She said she did. I asked if she could possibly be Sigrid Bergström. She said she was not, and that Sigrid Bergström had been dead for many years.

'But you are a relative?' I asked eagerly. 'Do you know this girl?'

I showed her the photograph. She shook her head to both questions. 'I am from Rattvik. No, I do not know her. I am sorry.'

We turned to leave, and my eyes fell on a yellow vase. It was not Karin's. It was not the same shape, and the yellow was deeper, but I bought it. There was a chance I'd get the opportunity to give it to her. On the base were the words: Siljan Keramics. The initials were nearly right. K.G. instead of K.B. I turned back to the woman. 'Karin?' I asked.

She smiled. 'Yes. Karin Gottberg.'

As we got back in the car, Eija murmured: 'She would not recognise the girl, Owen, now that she has a moustache.'

I nearly ran back to explain, but Eija was already moving off.

The next left-hander took us down towards the lake. During odd moments on curves I could see the water ahead. On our right we found Siljansgrden.

We drove in beneath an archway of birch branches, and over cobbles large enough to be called rocks. Eija stopped in front of a large red wooden building, with high steps up to its door. The porch was deep and the door was open. There was a bell push on the door frame. We pressed it on the way in. The hall was wide and deep and cool, dark, time-worn woodwork lining the walls, and a wooden staircase mounting from the rear. There was a folk-pattern rug covering the floor, so bright and so clean that I was afraid to venture my feet on it.

To the right, a tall, carved, old dresser stood against the wall, its horizontal surface covered with folders and leaflets that laid out the attractions of the district. Its back was criss-crossed with green tape, and into it were fitted the corners of photographs, cards, cuttings, all relating to Siljansgřden. One of the photographs was of a man and a woman, poised, their hands linked in typical folk-dance posture.

I cannot say what the man was wearing, except that it was yellow and black. But the young woman, small beside her partner and wearing spectacles, was dressed in exactly the same costume as Karin wore in my picture, except that she wore a white, starched cap instead of Karin's red ribbon.

'Look at this!' I cried, and a quiet voice at my elbow, in good English, said:

'That is my husband and myself. We are folk dancers.'

I turned. It was the same young woman. I produced my photograph. She smiled and nodded. 'The young lady was born not far from here. But she did not have the — '

'Not far?' I asked quickly, not wishing to discuss moustaches. I showed her the blue leaflet of Siljan Runt, which had on its front a map of Lake Siljan. 'Can you say how far?'

She took up a ballpoint pen and drew a circle, its centre Leksand. It was perhaps thirty kilometres across.

'In that area,' she said, nodding her certainty.

I just stood there, looking at it. We were so close. I realised that my behaviour might be strange. She was saying:

'And now. Can I help you? I am Signe Keys. My husband is Kenneth. Do you wish for accommodation?'

And so we came to Siljansgården. We were accepted and enfolded by its centuries-old peace, and I felt that I had come home. I had never seen any place like it, but it seemed that I had belonged there, and that I should not have left it. Gently, the atmosphere urged me never to leave it again.

Eija, because I was not attending, booked us two rooms. Accommodation was hard-pressed. She had a room upstairs in a reasonably modern hutment, probably as recent as 1700. I was downstairs in a sixteenth century log building they called a *Gammelloftet*, with outside, steep stairs to the upper rooms. I had a four-foot-high door into my room and a foot-high lintel I had to step over. They allowed for snow in those days; the whole building was lifted a foot from the ground on piles. Inside, the room was lined with modern pine, small and narrow, with a washbasin in an alcove and a modern Swedish bed that was soft and comfortable. The window was tiny, and I had to bend to look out of it.

Signe Keys had said that dinner was at 6.30. I washed and changed and met Eija in the lounge, where she was trying one of the ancient chairs, which were carved out of solid four-feet chunks of tree trunk. A few people drifted in, and we nodded to each other, and smiled. We all sat, and I couldn't understand what we were waiting for.

Then a man came in, and I knew at once he was Kenneth Keys. He wore a black jacket and a tie. Nobody else wore ties. He stood, with hands held before him, as though about to clap, and made an announcement in Swedish. Then he turned to me, before Eija could translate, his smile enveloping me.

'We have an English visitor with us tonight,' he said, in English slightly tinted with an Irish accent. 'I was just explaining that we are having asparagus soup,' he told me, 'followed by roast beef and gateau. Wine is available, if you wish it.'

It was that sort of hotel. Well, not a hotel, really. The translation, Signe Keys told me later, was Siljan Homestead. The grounds were scattered with hutments and chalets, all rescued from the distant past. I grinned at him as he ushered the others upstairs to the dining room.

He said: 'You *are* Owen Tanner?'

I said I was.

'Then there is something for you, in the hall. A motorcyclist left you a camera tripod. He said you might be needing it. I like to use a monopod myself.'

# 11

No doubt the beef was excellent, and with the soup we had soft, unleavened bread, plastered with gorgonzola, but the meal was spoiled for me. The mood had been shattered. I had been reminded that I wasn't there to enjoy myself.

Eija chattered. It was as she'd been when we first met. She chattered with a happy intensity, and the fact that Laurie had managed to trace us did not seem to upset her. But that had been a big pistol in his fist.

We went down to coffee in the lounge. The decor was very old, the woodwork inlaid, and there was a spinning-wheel in the corner by the raised, open fireplace. A log fire crackled in it pungently, in spite of the sun outside, but I was not comforted. Kenneth Keys brought me the tripod and laid it across my knees. There was no message.

Afterwards we walked down to the lake, and I told Eija my theory of why Laurie had taken the tripod from the Saab.

'And why should he return it?' she asked. Her arm was in mine. We must have looked

231

like two contented lovers strolling in the soft, clean air.

'He's telling me he no longer wishes to be treated as a busker. As we say in English thrillers, he's blown his cover. And he's telling me he's here.' If I needed him? Him and his gun! I didn't voice the thought.

We came down to the lake. Islands drifted out in the water, chunky outcrops of rock with their surfaces completely covered by pines. There was a small wooden jetty with a bench seat at its farthest reach, forming one side of a harbour for about twenty boats. Young people were scrambling on three of them, preparing them or stowing things away. We turned to the left, walking the strand between the scattered trees. The air was very still, and a long way away I heard a child laugh shrilly.

The sun was still high. There was nothing to do but allow the sanity to soak into your bones, and I was angry with it, because every tree could have hidden a watcher and every distant thrum of a motorcycle engine could have been Laurie's. And here I could sense the proximity of Karin.

We retraced our steps to the jetty and walked out onto it. A woman was airing a rough-haired dachshund. We stood by the bench seat, and watched one of the motorboats easing out into the lake. There was laughter across the water. Distantly, a tiny red spot moved across behind the islands, and I could hear the put-put of its outboard motor.

The air could not have been more clear, but I could barely see the opposite side of the lake. It was a grey line, crouching on the horizon.

'She distinctly said,' I told Eija, 'that she could see her chalet across the lake.' With her back to her friend Koch Karl something, she could see it through the star in the cross.

'Then it was not from here.' Her voice was comforting. The peace was in it. 'It must be four miles across at this point.'

'We'll have to look elsewhere.'

'Yes.' She tugged at my arm. 'Tomorrow.'

I was obscurely glad that it was not from there. It was no place for violence. Then, in the shocked realisation that I'd assumed it had to end with violence, I shuddered.

'You're cold,' she said quickly.

'I'm all right.'

'We'll go back now.'

It was ridiculous that I should not feel warm. The time was a little after eight, and the sun still had power. We strolled back up the slope to Siljansgården. I didn't want that walk to end.

'I think I'll take a shower,' she said.

'They've got showers?'

'You do not listen, Owen, that is your trouble. In the *flertalet*. She told us that.'

'So she did.' I grinned at her, and she went off to fetch her towel and things.

I tried to shake free of the cold foreboding, and decided it was time I justified my claim to being a photographer. It concentrates the mind. I had my tripod, now, after all, and the sunset over the lake promised to be worth capturing. Corny old sunsets, but that was my mood. There'd still be a couple of hours before it occurred. I went to get what I'd need.

The Canon with the 50mm lens, I decided. I took the tripod in one hand, walked round to the front of the main building, and turned to mount the stairs to the reception porch. From there I'd have a clear view over the fall of the gardens, with the lake glinting as a V between the trees farther down. Later, I'd walk, with Eija, down to the water.

I was not surprised to see Dick Kent sitting at the large round table on the lawn. He had his back to me, and seemed to have a tray with a coffee pot and one cup. I didn't want Kent, but the sunset was no more inevitable. He sat in pale slacks and a roll-neck silken pullover, like a blunt and alien accent in the landscape.

I walked down to him, placed the tripod on the table under his eyes, and sat beside him. I could not sit opposite him, because the stone table was eight feet across. Eight feet would not have been enough, anyway.

'It's fascinating to think,' he observed, 'that this stone was turning in a windmill four hundred years ago.'

It was a foot and a half thick, and the square hole in the centre was implanted with blue and yellow pansies. The Swedes seemed obsessed with those colours; I never saw any other.

'Probably a watermill,' I said. 'It's so big.'

'Have you looked round the place? It's wonderful. Every building is made from wood.'

He was waiting for me to cut short the formalities, challenging my nerves. 'I'm in the *Gammelloftet*,' I told him.

'Comfortable?'

'Very.'

'I'm at the Green Hotel.'

I reached for my pipe, which was still holding together. He moved the tripod an inch with his finger.

'I had to talk to you, Owen, before you

meet her.' He smiled. 'As you will.'

'I could have managed without your advice.'

He grimaced. The lowering sun bit into the planes of his face. 'We grate together like . . . like this millstone must have done on its mate,' he said.

'Where did you get the coffee?' I asked, wondering which of his stones was supposed to be on top.

'There's a café. There, the one with the turf roof, by the gate.'

I moved to rise. Suddenly I had to see the turf roof. Karin had spoken of her chalet. 'We had a storage shed with a turf roof.'

'Don't go now,' he said quickly, almost in appeal. Then he added, more serenely: 'They're closed, I think.'

I relaxed in the chair. My pipe would not draw.

'There's something we've got to get very clear, Owen.'

'Everything seems quite clear to me.'

He refused to be rattled. 'You obviously realise we've been using you to get close to Niels Bergh. You're interested in meeting your wife. All right, so the two things have worked together, because Bergh and Karin are together. You haven't been easy to keep in touch with.' He was rueful. 'One hell of a job tracing you to here.'

So Eija hadn't informed him. I smiled at him. Suddenly he was one hell of a fellow. 'You could have taken me into your confidence.'

'I've worked with you!' he exploded. 'It's why we couldn't. Damn it all — tell you to go to A and you'd go to B. Tell you to go to A and B, and off you'd go chasing to C, on some wildly romantic knight-errant jag of your own. No, mate, it had to be more subtle.'

'Subtle?' I thought about that. 'Such as planting Eija Larsson on me?'

'I didn't plant her on you. What're you talking about?'

I stared at him. He wasn't lying, there'd be no point at this stage. 'Then in what way subtle?'

'We threw a few obstacles in your way, made a few threats. Owen Tanner went running in the way we wanted.'

Nobody, it seemed, had any great regard for me. 'So say what you've got to.'

'We know you're getting very close. We don't know your business with your wife — that's your own affair.'

'Well . . . thank you for that.'

'We simply want that necklace — all of it.'

'For God's sake!' I burst out. 'The Finns are prepared to pay for it. You told me that. But no, you had to get it back the hard way. Two people have died. No, don't you try to wave me down. You can hear me out. Two lives. And you're weighing 'em against a bit of blackmail, which they're ready to pay, anyway. You make me sick.'

'But not a *bit* of blackmail. They're reckoning on half a million.'

'Pounds?'

'Kroner. But don't tell Bergh.' He made a spluttering sound that served as his laugh. 'He might settle for half of that.'

'Get it down low enough, and those two lives'd be worth nothing,' I said in disgust.

'Don't try to be funny, Owen. And anyway it was robbery, and now it's blackmail. Extortion, more like. It's illegal, so it's a police matter.'

'You smug bastard.'

'And to tell you the truth, I'm in line for promotion. Do this right for me, Owen — '

'You hypocritical prick!' I shouted.

'Language! You'll offend the Swedes.'

'Oh, mate,' I said, 'you're going the right way to get my co-operation. Just talk on, and maybe I'll poke you in the mouth.'

'From now on you'll be watched every minute,' he said placidly. 'And you'll behave.

Just point us at Bergh, and we'll take it from there.'

'And anyway,' I said, not having troubled to listen to his platitudes, 'what about that theft of the settings! I've never heard of such a stupid, botched-up business. Bergh'd got the stones. All they'd have to do was offer a reward for them. The same money, if necessary. No need for getting some poor bleeder knocked on the head to snatch the settings. Just advertise, through an agent.'

He stretched out his legs. His smile told me I was a minor irritation. 'You never did have any imagination, Owen. That way, the Finns would be calling the tune, and Bergh'd be suspicious and back off. This way, he's got the lot, and he's got nowhere else he can unload it all. But he can call the tune, arrange the pick-up, and the handover. It makes him more . . . tractable. The Finns are ready to go along with him — anything to get it all back in one piece. But I'm not.'

I noticed that a few minutes before it'd been 'we', but now it was 'I'. Thought he'd got his promotion already.

'Right,' I said. 'You can count on me. I'll do my best to contact Karin. What I've got to say to her is personal, and doesn't include any chit-chat about stones and settings and things like that. But if the subject crops up . . . I'll put in a good word for you, Dick. I'll tell her you're a reliable man, and Bergh can trust you to kick him in the balls when he's not looking, and trample all over him if there's a sight of jewels or settings or both. Or a sight of promotion. How'd that suit you?'

His jaw was working. Slowly, with stiff, finely-controlled movements, he felt in his pocket and produced a pack of cigarettes. He opened it, and it was empty. I laughed, and held up my pipe. I tried it, and it was drawing again, so I lit it and blew smoke over him.

'You bugger this for me, Owen, and I'll kill you,' he said softly.

'I happen to know the agent the Finns are using,' I told him. 'Think we might work up a deal, Dick?'

His face was distorted when he got to his feet. But he was a copper, and that overrode it all. He stood with his clenched fist resting on the top of the stone table, and spoke thickly, from deep in his throat.

'There's something else.'

I'd had enough. 'What else can there be?'

'She's waiting for you.'

'Who — '

'Karin is waiting, down at the lake.'

I reached past him and snatched up the

tripod. 'Damn you,' I whispered. I was close to hitting him with it.

Then I was running, the tripod clasped in my right hand, the camera bumping on a short strap against my chest.

'Watch it!' he called after me weakly.

Then I slowed to a stroll. Karin would wait for me. It was what she'd come there for, to wait for me.

I stopped. The effort to do so was a great strain, but I stopped in order to give my brain time to catch up. She was down at the lake, and she was waiting, when, before, it had been frantic flight or brief, secret messages. This meeting was off-centre, and the machinery was running wild. Or running down. She had wanted me to come to her, of that I was certain. If she'd wanted me to stay at home, she could have left me a note. 'I am sorry, Owen, but I do not love you.' Something simple like that. It would have kept me at home.

But now I would be told. I walked on slowly.

The sun was low over the water. In Sweden it takes a long time for the sun to decide to call it a day. Four people whom I recognised were walking up from the lake. They said it was a beautiful evening. They said it in Swedish, so I could only guess and

241

smile. The evening was perfect.

The road swung left at the bottom, under the trees, where there was a kiosk. It was now closed. The shadows were long and purple from the pines, the air breathing a gentle tang from them. The harbour was quiet, the boats barely moving at their moorings. A boy swooped past me on a pedal cycle and leaned into the corner, and then I saw her.

She was sitting with her back to me on the bench seat at the end of the jetty. The water moved like golden oil, and she was cast in silhouette, but the shape of her I knew. I felt breathless, my heart pounding. I was a young man again, meeting my first date, aware that any wrong move or wrong word would repulse her. The silhouette, I knew intimately; the person was a stranger.

She did not turn at the sound of my feet on the wooden slats. The clear water was brown, I saw, brown with the dye of birch bark and pine needles. I stood in front of her, but she did not raise her eyes. Her right hand was lightly holding the rope attached to a small, red rowing boat with an outboard engine clamped to its stern. I sat beside her, laying the tripod symbolically between us. I sensed that she had to have a distance between us, however small.

'You've come to talk?' I asked softly.

Then she turned to face me, and my fingers tightened on the tripod. On her lips there was not one trace of the gentle patience that I knew. They were firm, thin and pale. Her cheeks were hollow, with red blotches hectic on her cheekbones. Her eyes were dark and sunken, and there was something in them that caught my breath, a cold depth in what had been such beautiful eyes, an ugliness. She was not looking at Owen, her husband, she was looking at something else, and I felt soiled, not fit to be there. Her lips moved. It seemed an effort.

'You look well, Owen.'

'And you,' I lied. 'It's been a long time . . .' Or so it seemed.

'Very handsome,' she decided, squinting her eyes at me as though it dazzled her. 'Did I ever tell you that?'

'A thousand times. I never believed you.'

'The very first time — ' She caught her lower lip in her teeth. I thought she was trying to control tears, and looked away. I could never stand her tears, but they had been rare, so I should really have treasured them. I didn't know what to say.

The motorboat I'd seen moving out was roaring along the lake, the other side of the islands. Sea birds screamed over the pines, disputing their roosts, I supposed, now that

243

the sun was going down.

I said, 'I realise you asked me to turn back, Karin. But you know I couldn't do that.'

'I'm sure you couldn't.' There was an unexpected snap to the words.

'I had a few clues, though.'

'You've followed them well. I wonder why they threw you out of the police, Owen.'

I persisted, though she seemed unresponsive. 'I've bought you a yellow vase, from Siljan Keramics. I know it's not the same — '

Her head had jerked round. Her eyes glowed. 'You can put it in the same place, where the other was.' She had spat it at me.

I could understand nothing. I spoke gently. 'You could do that yourself.'

There was silence. The jetty creaked. The silence was heavier in the scream of the birds.

'I saw you, that first time, in the Rainbow Club in Birmingham,' she murmured. 'You had your camera.'

'I was replacing their regular man, who was sick.' It was a lie. I'd had my camera with me, and I'd been looking for beautiful faces, for that certain combination of soft planes that a photographer dreams of. But lies did not matter, only a smooth flow of progressive conversation.

244

She said, 'But no. He was there. He'd already taken a picture of us, at the table.' Lies mattered to Karin.

'I wasn't interested in the man you were with.'

'Lennie . . . I don't remember his other name. I'd picked him up at the bar.' Her tone was dismissive, as though the memory shamed her.

I didn't know what she was saying, or trying to. She seemed locked in a memory she was trying to cling to. If so, her voice should have been soft and dreamy, if the memory evoked nostalgic pleasure. But the edge of her voice was sharply slicing it into inhuman scenes.

'I soon got rid of him,' I said.

'Did you? I had the idea that I did.'

I laughed, recalling the scene. It was difficult to laugh. There was that romantic idea I was pursuing at the time, that I could break through into the lucrative world of the fashion photographer. If I could only find the right model.

'I came over to your table,' I reminded her. 'I told buster — '

'Lennie.'

' . . . that I wanted to buy you a drink. He definitely wasn't happy.'

'You nearly started a fight.'

'He was bigger than me. I told him you were my cousin.'

'Did you? I don't remember that.'

'I told him I'd push his face in.'

'Did you really do that?' she asked coldly. 'I asked him not to make a scene.'

I'd been high on professional excitement. I'd seen Karin's slender hands modelling gloves, her golden head modelling hats, her slender body . . .

'I had to have you, Karin.'

'That's what I thought you meant.'

'As a model. I thought that together we'd hit the top.'

'As a model? But you never asked me to model for you, so how can I believe that?'

'Plans change. I'd met you . . . and it all happened so quickly.'

'So terribly quickly,' she agreed.

'You swept me off my feet,' I said defensively. Her voice had been sour.

'Did I, Owen? As I recall that time, it was you doing the sweeping.'

I'd been going along with it, keeping it going to please her. But she didn't sound pleased. I was uneasy, not understanding, and we were in dispute.

'However it was,' I said desperately. 'Who cares?'

'Perhaps I do.'

'Can we talk about *now*? I must know — '

She raised her chin. The sun was red, but there was going to be no real sunset. A line of grey cloud was crowding the sun on the horizon, and the motor boat scattered the lake into slivers of green and gold.

'I was under the impression,' she said to the sky, 'that it was I who picked you up.'

Was she trying deliberately to belittle me? 'I was more handsome than him. You admitted that.' Trying levity.

She nodded. 'There was that, of course.'

'I've got to talk about other things,' I said tersely.

'But what more can you want?' she asked, turning to me suddenly. 'You know very well where to go.'

'Home?' I asked in disgust.

'You *know*.' Her eyes were swimming with pain.

'I don't know what you're saying,' I said angrily. 'You talk a lot of fantasy about the time we first met, when all I want to know is why I'm here. What do you want from me, Karin?'

'No more than you are.'

'Oh Lord! Listen, please.'

'I think I've heard enough.'

'But I've heard nothing!' I shouted.

247

My voice fluttered the birds on the island. They called back.

Then she stared at me with naked hatred. I searched desperately behind her eyes for something that wasn't rejection, because that wasn't what I'd come all that way for, and I'd had about as much as I could handle. But there was nothing there I could cling to.

'You're not leaving?' I gasped.

She had risen to her feet. There was, in her movement, no touch of her former lithe grace. It was simply tense with purpose.

'There's no more to say.'

'There's everything to say. I don't understand. I don't know what's going on.'

She drew on the painter. The small boat bobbed beneath her. She was not looking at me. 'By God, how you can lie,' she said, not far from a sob. 'Four years, and every day a lie!'

She made a movement to step into the boat. I touched her at last, laid a hand on her arm. She whirled on me. 'Don't touch me!' she choked.

There was so much revulsion in her voice that I snatched back my hand, as though her flesh was on fire. I watched her step into the boat. It bobbed. She seemed unsteady. She snatched at the draw-line, and the engine fired unevenly.

She did not look back at me. The boat pointed its nose between the two islands, and she went into the dazzle of the sun, disturbing the birds. As she passed between the islands I wanted to shout after her, but something was hard in my throat.

The sea birds screamed and cried, but not as furiously as I was screaming.

# 12

Eija came to me from the shadows beneath the trees. I had been moving blindly up the slope from the lake. She took the tripod from me, and linked her arm with mine, drawing me close.

'You're shaking,' she whispered.

'Did you hear?'

I felt, rather than saw, the negative movement of her head. 'I was too far away. But I heard you cry out.' She looked up into my face. 'She hurt you.'

'I don't know what she did. I'm confused. I don't understand anything.' I said it with my fists tightly clenched against the universal enemy, ignorance.

We had reached the entrance to the homestead. The sky was dark, as dark as it would get, the cloud bank having finally consumed the sun.

'Where can we talk?' I asked, because I had to or go mad.

'There's a TV room. Underground. You can smoke there.'

Everywhere there were signs: *Rökning Förbjuden*. There was no building that was anything but wood.

'There'll be people there,' I said.

'We'll see.'

She took me through the lounge, and down the stairs instead of up to the dining room. We walked a narrow passage. There were two TV rooms in a kind of U, in the first a dozen people in the easy chairs, watching an American thriller with Swedish sub-titles. The other was empty, the protesting tyres and frequent gunfire apparently being irresistible. We sat at a round table, side by side on a settee. There were books on the walls, wild flowers in a vase, and a silent TV set.

I lit my pipe. Eija was watching me, waiting for me to speak, her eyes melting with concern.

I told her every word that I could remember. She nodded, not interrupting, her eyes large.

'The only thing I can think,' I said, 'is that she's no longer sane.' I was miserable with the thought. If she was mentally ill, then that would chop the foundations from under me. I'd have no defence, and offence would be futile. My mind groped for alternatives, but came up with nothing I could face.

'There could be another explanation,' she said.

'What?'

'I don't know. I only feel there has to be something.'

I put my head back. I was exhausted. I felt Eija take the pipe from my fingers, and sleep swept over me. Some time later I reached for my pipe in a dream . . .

'Come,' said Eija. 'It is late.'

I got to my feet groggily. The TV in the other room was silent, and when we walked through the lights were low, and Kenneth Keys was tidying the room.

'*Godnatt*,' he said.

We murmured to him, and went on through. The night air was crisp. We mounted the outside stairway to Eija's room, and when she opened the window a dog was barking far away. I fancied that in the still night I could hear the sea birds, but maybe the shrill protest was inside me.

When I turned, she was sitting on the edge of the bed in bra and pants. I glanced away, and back. She was pouting.

'I can't think.' I waved a hand wildly. 'Can't rest.'

'Sit here, Owen.' Patting the bed beside her.

But I was unsettled, and pacing the floor.

'She rejected me. That's it. Flatly and calmly she told me to go to hell.'

'It need not be so.' Patient Eija.

I hadn't told her the last few words I'd discovered on the back of the photograph. *If you love me.*

'And me . . . ' I said wildly. 'What did I do? I just sat there like a dumb idiot, and couldn't find the right words. Couldn't find *any* words. Oh Christ, what was the matter with me?'

'The matter,' she said briskly, 'was that she used a hammer to you, when she could have done it with a few persuasive words.'

'Done what? What?' I demanded.

'Do try to look at it calmly. Just think back. All the time you've been given clues to lead you on, but all the time she's been telling you to go back, because she's been afraid for you, this Karin of yours — '

'Mine!'

'Karin — she clearly feels you could be in danger, and she has the fear for you.'

I stood still, by the window, looking at her. She seemed like a small, lost child, sitting there, forlorn and miserable. She was offering me something, retrieving something.

'But now she hates me.'

Eija shrugged. 'With you, she puts on the act. You're such a fool, you never see the truth. She's been so good for you, Owen. That is how you see it. At that time she was what for you had need.'

Now she was on her feet, as agitated as me, and her English flying wild. She came to me and seized my arms, holding me so that I couldn't avoid her intensity.

'But all the time . . . oh, you dear, sweet idiot, Owen . . . all the time it has been from her something cool and calculated. You say to me that she has helped you — thrust you — controlled you the way it is best. But I have the idea . . . ' She cocked her head. 'The idea that all the while she said you would do it if you loved her.' Noticed the flicker of my eyes. 'If you love me, you will do this, Owen, or do that.' Oh, the scorn in her voice! 'But she would know the time with you had the limits. Until Niels Bergh was coming out of prison. So you filled that time for her. You amused her. You'd be like a . . . like a broken doll to her. A repair here and there. It saved her getting bored.'

'No, no!' I tried to shake myself free.

'Listen! Listen, damn you, to me. You cannot keep running from it. Everybody tells it to you, and you do not listen. They tell you there is danger, to turn back. They tell you . . . *she* tells you . . . not to follow her, and you, you stubborn, ridiculous fool, you do not listen to anybody but your own idiotic . . . ' She had tears in her eyes, but no hand free to dash them away. 'And

254

now . . . will you not *see*, Owen . . . now she is impatient with you. If hatred will turn you away, she gives you hatred. And if you will not listen . . . ' A sob, but she controlled it. 'If you are not listening to that, what will she do next to stop you?'

'No!' I said violently.

'Oh Owen . . . please . . . '

I got my arms free. I gripped my fingers into her shoulders and thrust my face close to hers. 'No!' I shouted into her face, and I thrust her away so violently that she stumbled the few paces back, and fell full length on the bed.

'You don't know,' I tried. 'You can't . . . ' But the words wouldn't come, and my violence had suddenly drained me.

She said nothing, hair awry and her huge, frightened eyes following my every move and gesture.

I moved to her and sat beside her. She lay, looking up at me, wide-eyed. I reached down and drew her up, and put an arm round her shoulders.

'I hurt you,' I whispered. 'I'm sorry.'

'It doesn't hurt.'

'I was angry. You can't know . . . '

She drew my head down to her breast. I was low, way down at rock bottom. 'You can't know,' I mumbled, 'what we had together. She . . . she . . . the things she did for me. Oh dear Lord!'

Somehow her bra was no longer there, and the tears that ran between her breasts might not have been hers. I sobbed, and I babbled, and everything that Karin had been to me came out in disjointed and broken fragments, all of it poured between the soft receptive breasts of Eija, the Eija I hadn't wanted to hurt, but who murmured softly to me, encouraging me to hurt her again, over and over, if only the pain could be shared. Until I was exhausted with the telling, and she stronger for the listening, and we were in each other's arms. There was nowhere else for either of us.

Nothing can ever be like the first time. We came together as though we'd been away too long, and the journeying had ended, and there was time now to savour the eternity of it.

Afterwards I lay silent. She was not asleep. Fingers crept over my chest. The night was quiet. Distantly, a bird cried, and now the scream was far away from me. I was empty, no pain, no fear.

Softly, she whispered, 'In the morning, we will try to find the church that Karin mentioned. Would you like to do that, Owen?'

'Yes. I'd like that.'

She kissed me on the lips. Her thigh stirred against mine. There was peace enough, but room for ecstacy.

Very early in the morning we walked beside the lake, a mist barely clearing the islands, walked hand in hand, and nothing was said of Karin or Niels Bergh or the Tammela Necklace. Or of my fear.

When we returned to the homestead I could not see Signe Keys anywhere. Over breakfast I asked her husband if I could speak to her, and Signe came to us in the lounge.

There was a cross with a star in it, and Karin had said I would be able to see the chalet through it. Crosses meant churches.

'We're looking for churches,' I said, and Signe nodded. Visitors often looked for churches.

'There is a church at Leksand and one at Rattvik, which is north from here, around the lake,' she said.

I produced the blue leaflet, Siljan Runt. She herself had drawn the circle.

'It has to be in that area,' I said.

'Then it must be the one at Leksand.'

'Where it is possible to see the other side of the lake?' I was trying to make it very clear.

She smiled at my emphasis. 'Then it *is* Leksand.'

'Has it got a cross with a star in it?' I asked eagerly.

She looked disappointed. Helping people clearly made her very happy. 'I'm sorry . . . there are many crosses. It is very beautiful there.' She smiled again. 'You can go and see for yourself.'

Eija went to fetch the car from the car park at the side. I went to get my camera equipment, and to turn back the bedcovers, as though I had slept there. I took the tripod and my Canon, with the big zoom lens, which I could use as a sort of telescope on full magnification.

Eija was parked on the cobbles.

'I'm ready,' I told her.

'Are you sure you want this, Owen?'

'I don't think it's got anything to do with what I want.'

She tried not to frown, and drove away. 'You'll go to your grave a stubborn fool,' she said, but with affection.

I shook my head. I didn't feel stubborn. I felt like a drowning man swimming for a raft, which might not support him even if he reached it.

The church at Leksand has its own approach road. You drive past the Tourist

Bureau, and keep going. On the left is a wide, open expanse of public parkland, with a row of trees beyond it, clothing the cliff down to the lake. It was quiet. We drew in to the car park, and there were only three cars in it. One of them was the blue Citroen.

We got out and I looked around. Only the very top of the church spire was visible beyond the trees surrounding it. I could see nobody.

'What day is it?' I asked.

'Monday.' She was standing by the Alfa, her eyes not leaving me.

'That explains it, then.'

The locals would have made their calls the day before. Now, there was only the odd tourist — the odd murderer.

'You'd better stay here,' I told her.

'But why? You can see he's here. This is the Citroen.'

'They'll be here to observe, I'd say. To see whether I spot the chalet.'

'It'll be safe?' Her eyes sharp.

'Certainly.'

'Then why shouldn't I be with you?' she asked with simple logic.

'You're like a child. Why, why, why.'

'I simply wanted to know.'

'It'd be better if you're with the car,' I said. I grinned, lightening the atmosphere.

'In case we have to make a fast getaway.'

She nodded, not believing and not accepting. I fitted the zoom lens to the camera, took up the tripod, and walked round the end of the car park.

I was facing the church. There was a long and wide gravelled driveway to it, obviously not intended for cars because it was guarded by two troughs of purple and yellow pansies. The drive was flanked by tall and stately silver birches, and the owner of one of the other vehicles was just coming back to it, with a black poodle on a lead.

The church was a dazzle of pure white in the sun, topped by a black onion dome and a gold cross. I began to walk towards it. There were wrought-iron gates at the end of the drive, and then the churchyard spread out to my right, reaching beyond the far side of the church. Peace rested in the churchyard, and I began to walk the neat gravelled paths. I saw nobody. It was so quiet that I could hear the bees working. I saw no movement anywhere, and there were only random trees, and no high gravestones to hide behind.

Instead, there was carefully-trimmed grass, with small headstones or three-foot wrought-iron crosses, with different decorations to each. There were hundreds of little crosses, but if they had stars they'd be too low to look through. There were no graves, as I'd always known them. The dead had no cause to advertise their presence here; they were still alive in the affections of their loved ones. Each low headstone rested in a bed of planted flowers, and each cross, standing simply in the grass, had its vase of blooms. I walked. I forgot what I was looking for, and the fear had drained away.

The graveyard extended almost to the lake, only a stretch of grass and a few small trees guarding the fall of the cliff. Looking down, I could see that the cliff, here, was no more than thirty feet high. But it was clothed heavily with ancient trees, which reached high. This could not be the place. From nowhere on the opposite side of the lake would it have been possible to see the church through that barrier, and Karin had definitely said she could see the church from her chalet.

Somehow, I was relieved. If Bergh and Karin were here I could see no sign of them, and if this was not the place, then there could be no reason for me to be there, either, except to absorb the silence.

I turned to the right and walked the path beside the lake. I crossed a footbridge that straddled an incline down to the water's edge, and now I could hear the movement of water and the excited chirping of birds. I turned a corner round a high bank of wild roses, and located the sound. Beside the edge of the cliff, in a small clearing of its own, there was a monument consisting of a large round stone, four feet across, from the top of which water was bubbling gently. The birds were paddling in the film of water, drinking from it. I approached softly. I brought my camera up and wound it on to full focal length. It was only when the birds lifted in alarm, and I paused, that I realised I was standing with the cross almost at my left elbow.

I stood back. The cross was about eight feet high, in weather-beaten wood, with trefoil decoration at the extent of each arm. Cut through the centre of the topmost trefoil was a six-pointed star. Flowers surrounded its foot, but there was no dedication. To each side, ten feet away, there were white marble urns, also containing flowers, red geraniums and small yellow daisies. I approached the cliff edge, standing beside the star. Here, the trees had been cut away from the cliff. For a width of fifty feet, the fall to the wide path at the water's edge was grass-covered, and not quite vertical. This was the only place the cross would have been visible from across the water. I glanced behind. The church, too.

There had been movement in the trees behind me. They were closely planted just there, fifty feet back from the cliff. I looked, but I could have imagined it. In any event, the excitement was in me now, and everything was background to it. I turned back to the cross.

The star was over a foot above my head. All I could see through it was sky. But behind me the ground sloped steeply up to the path. I began to back away from the cross, my eyes on the star, watching the far bank of the lake gradually rise to it. The air was wonderfully clear. I realised I was able to see the cluster of trees across the water, and speckled red houses amongst them. It had to be one of those!

I backed. I felt the gravel path beneath my feet, but my eyes were on the star. Then I stepped up onto the rising grass again, and clearly, through the star, I could see the trees and the houses. But a movement of my head of only a foot sideways displaced the image through the star by about a hundred yards. The lake must have been two miles wide at that point. I had no marker. I stumbled, glancing down and back. I had nearly stepped into an arrangement of flowers in front of a low, rose-coloured headstone. In it, in gold letters, was cut the inscription:

Kock Karl Danielsson.

I had been a fool. Karin had said she'd stood with her back to Kock Karl Danielsson, and I'd imagined a friend, one alive. But I should have equated a cross with a churchyard, and guessed at a headstone. *This* was where Karin had stood, and from here, through the star in the cross, she had been able to see her chalet.

I stood with my back to the headstone and seized my tripod. The intention was to attach the camera, with the zoom lens at full focal length, and sight through the star. Then I could check that I had one specific chalet in the centre of my focusing screen, and finally establish its location.

I never completed the action.

There was a shout of rage behind me. I whirled round. Niels Bergh was running at me from the cover of the trees. He had a pistol in a two-handed grip, for steadiness, but you can't aim with such a grip if you run. He was charging at me through the neat barrier of headstones and crosses, which barely reached above his knees, scattering the wrought-iron and the flowers. I backed frantically. I held the tripod before my face, as though it might give me some protection.

Still running, still shouting his fury, he

fired. The shot whined past my head. I was stepping back towards the cross, and rapidly running out of ground. My senses seemed suddenly to become acutely attuned. I was aware than a woman stood where Bergh had started from, and that there was a flicker of red down a path on the edge of my vision. Bergh ran at me, and he fired again. I felt the bullet snatch at my jacket. The tall cross was now at my elbow, and I stood at the very edge of the drop, with nowhere else to go.

He fired once more. His feet pounded across the gravel path. He missed with that one, but every second the range was decreasing, and he could not continue to miss.

Eija's voice came crisply on the still air.

'*Stanna! Stanna, annars skjuter jag!*'

I risked one flickered glance at her. She stood firm, her small pistol in the same two-handed grip. But she was not moving, and she didn't wait for him to halt. In any event, he was so close, and his charge was so furious, that he could not have halted.

She fired. It seemed a puny little crack, compared with the bellow of his big automatic, but she got him in the leg. He faltered, his leg twisted, and he staggered. Then he was into me with his left shoulder down, taking me above the knees. I gasped as the pistol rammed into my left kneecap. Then we went over the edge, scrambling together, pitching down the grass slope and onto the verge beneath.

I had seen it as a grassed, cleared slope, but there were two stunted little trees in it. My leg twisted against one of them, and I went down the last ten feet head first. There was a line of rocks in the grass at the foot of the drop. I plunged into them, and then everything was an emptiness until I found myself raising my head and looking round, to place myself in this world.

I ached. My leg seemed to have been twisted, and my knee cried out in agony. The camera had dug into my chest on the way down. My head felt spongy and not firmly attached.

Beside me, Bergh was lying very still. The gun was still in his hand. I touched his wrist, an exploratory movement, and I wondered whether he was dead. Then I got to my feet, labouring at it. Somebody called my name. I looked up, and my head swam. Eija's red scarf around her neck was a spark of blood against the sky.

'Owen!'

'I'm all right.' Which was a straight lie.

'You can get back,' she called, waving to my left. 'Round the corner of the rocks.'

I stumbled around the outcrop. There was another of those cutaway slopes with another footbridge over it. At the water's edge the little red boat was bobbing. I fumbled my way up the slope, hearing Eija's running feet across the bridge. She came down to meet me. I'd been having difficulty with the twin ruts made by a tractor. She put a hand under my arm and round me, and I put mine about her shoulders. They were shaking.

'You're hurt.' She was almost whimpering.

'You're quite good with a pistol.'

'I didn't hit you!' A wail.

'No. You got him in the leg. I simply fell.'

We staggered up to the level of the path above. I was gasping with the pain and effort, and she still seized by shock.

'Karin was here, Eija.'

'I saw her. She made no move to stop him.'

'We've got to catch her. Now I can talk to her.' And no arguing this time. No playing around with emotional nostalgia.

'You can talk to nobody,' she said severely. 'You certainly cannot chase anybody.'

'But I've located the chalet.'

'You made that very clear. You made a childish punch at the air, like an idiotic footballer.'

'Where is she? Can you see her?'

She turned me. Way across the churchyard and nearly into the approach drive, I could see Karin running from me. She was a flicker of biscuit slacks through the trees, and a pale blue blouse.

'We've got to go after her,' I said. 'There's a village over there — '

'Västanvik,' she agreed. She had assisted me to a bench, a little back from the cross. My breath was easing, but my head throbbed. I touched my forehead. It was hot and tender.

'But you're not going there, Owen. The police cannot be far away. They'll know the location, now, and they'll follow her there. She's on her own, and they'll pick her up and search the chalet, and that will be the end of it.'

She couldn't see! 'But I've got to reach her before they do.'

'She can't get far, on her own.'

Then I heard the cough and splutter of the outboard motor firing. I stumbled across to the edge of the drop, my legs working a little better now. Beyond the outcrop of the rock the red boat came into view. Niels Bergh was looking back at me, his head turned, one leg thrust forward awkwardly. He raised his pistol, his face distorting as he saw me, and I stepped back quickly, but not before I'd noticed my tripod lying at his feet.

Eija caught me before I fell. Partly it was the sudden weight on the knee as I turned, which took support from me, partly the shock of realisation.

'The tripod!' I babbled.

'Easy, Owen. Take my arm.'

I half-crawled back to the bench. Everything had suddenly become appallingly clear.

'They've been using me as a bloody courier,' I croaked. 'Don't you see, they had the stones hidden in the tripod.'

'Quiet, now,' she said gently. 'Do not be upset.'

'Upset! Of course I'm upset. He wanted me to come here — his clues were leading me on. I was bringing them to him.'

'And . . . Karin?'

I stared at her.

'Why did she ask you to turn back?' Eija asked, nodding, forcing it into my brain with calm words. 'Why was she hating you so much last night, if you were no more than a delivery man?'

She knocked the breath out of me. No words came.

'Or would it be better for you, Owen, to accept that it is true, and that it is no more than hatred because you are you?'

'I'll . . . I'll . . . ' I tried to get up and walk away. Her fingers were like pincers in my arm.

'But what you say is ridiculous, anyway,' she claimed. 'No . . . listen. Listen!' she hissed with intensity. 'Perhaps they *are* hidden in the tripod. Somewhere they would have to be hidden. It does not matter. They can't have based everything on the assumption you'd bring it with you, even if you did follow her. If necessary, they could simply have returned for it. Perhaps she left hurriedly, at a time when you had it with you.'

I nodded. It was so. My heart slowed and I was more calm.

'And in any event, there have been so many chances for them to take it from you. They would not have waited for you to get this far. But yes . . . ' She stopped, and she looked beyond me for the thought. 'Yes, if they had taken it from you earlier, you would perhaps have thought as you do now, that you are no more than a courier for them — and you would have returned home. You see, Owen, there is something more. It is *you* they have wanted to come this far. Or he would surely not have needed to shout out with such hatred, and fire three shots at you.'

Why did she always have to rescue me from myself? Why did she have to fasten the hatred on Bergh, and allow me to keep my faith in Karin alive?

I got to my feet quickly, more securely. She allowed me to do it, and made no protest when I went forward again to the cliff edge.

The boat was moving out slowly, its engine misfiring. At that speed, it'd take him a good hour to get back to the other side. I thought I could locate the chalet, without any more help from the cross. Karin would head there and wait for him.

I turned back to Eija. She was standing, her shoulder bag hooked forward by one thumb, with something stiff and formal about her stance. I'd not encountered that expression before, and I thought she seemed pale.

'We've got to find the chalet before he gets there,' I said.

She shook her head slowly, gravely, distress in her eyes. 'There comes a time when I cannot let you go on. I have watched you race from one idiotic action to the other. Now it must stop. Owen Tanner, I am going to place you under protective custody.'

The words meant nothing. They raced round in my mind, seeking identity. Her hand slid into her shoulder bag. I couldn't believe it.

'Like hell you are!' I roared, and I began to run towards her, trying to reach her before the gun appeared.

The muted thrum of a motorcycle engine did not immediately register. I thought it was in my mind. I ran, and her hand remained quietly in the bag. I ran until the horn shrilled, and the bike was nearly on me. I skidded to a stop. Laurie pulled up a foot short. He was wild.

'Y' let him get away, you stupid bleeder,' he shouted.

'I couldn't . . . he's heading across the lake.' My eyes darted from him to Eija, then back.

He'd got there by riding down the paths. He was hauling his bike round, stabbing furiously at the gravel.

'I'll be waitin' for him!' he cried.

I spoke quickly, before he worked that throttle. 'Take me with you.'

He paused, his head turned, his eyes blank.

'Take me. I know the place.'

He suddenly smiled. He looked past me, to Eija. Thought flickered behind his eyes.

'Jump on then.'

I sprang for the rear of the dual seat. Eija

shouted out, 'Owen . . . no.'

The camera was a hard, awkward lump between Laurie and my chest. I tore the strap over my head savagely and threw the camera on the grass at Eija's feet. Then I saw that she'd brought out her hand, empty, from the bag, and was making a clutching gesture in the air, as though I might be close enough to reach. But Laurie was away. I grabbed for him, nearly going backwards over the rear wheel. The bike plunged, and gravel sprayed.

'Owen!' she shouted.

I looked back once more. She was watching me go, but her hand was already reaching down for the camera.

Laurie took the perimeter path around the churchyard, the lake to our right. At the end it swung away and circled the church. It narrowed, one-person width now. There was a tiny wrought-iron gate, but it was open, and Laurie skimmed through it with an inch to spare each side. A man in a habit and hood called out something, but then we were away, zig-zagging through the trees, and emerged at the top end of the car park.

The blue Citroen had gone. A police car was coming in fast along the road beside the open park. Laurie turned away from them, then leaned at speed into a fork I hadn't noticed. It was signposted: Tällberg.

I glanced back. He was up to fifty, with a T-junction coming up fast. The police weren't following, I realised.

'Turn right here,' I shouted. 'Right! Back through Leksand and over the bridge.'

He braked hard, flicked down a couple of gears, and turned left.

'What're you doing?' I bellowed into the air-stream.

He half turned his head. 'He's mine. You ain't gonna get in the way.'

'You're crazy. Turn round, you damned fool.'

The air rushed past my head, whipping my naked eyes. They streamed, and I could barely see the road. He opened the throttle, and we were into the twisting stretch. Trees flickered past me, and he threw the bike into the corners. My knees plunged down towards the road surface at every turn, pain throbbing through the left one.

'Dump y' somewhere,' he shouted, the words tossed away. 'Keep yer outa the way.'

'You'll lose him, you fool.'

'There's time.' Then he lifted his head, and half turned his chin. The words spilled back at me quite clearly.

'D'you think I'd come this far, and miss out?'

I clung to him. The ride was now a nightmare. The engine note was a howl.

'What do you mean?' I shouted, making each word separate and distinct. 'Stop and tell me what you mean.'

It was futile. He attacked the next bend. Then I guessed what he must have meant. Miss out on the necklace.

I blinked my eyes rapidly, trying to disperse the tears, and deliberately stared past his shoulder into the rush of air. For one second I had a clear view of the road ahead. There was a left-hander coming up, and we were on the outside of it. He grated a gear, going down through the box, and I felt the brakes bite. The front wheel dipped as the pads gripped the disc brake. He leaned hard over to his left, and with an effort I flung all my weight to the right.

It felt as though I was lifting the whole weight of the bike with my back and legs. We maintained the turn for a second, and then we began to weave. I threw myself over even further, and flame burned through my knee. The weave became a wobble. My face reached down to kiss the tarmac. The wheel beneath me locked. He tried to snatch the front tyre from the grass verge, and then the dual seat hit me as we plunged up into the trees, and frantically I threw myself sideways, away from the tumbling mass of metal, and rolled between the pines with my arms around my head.

Then it became very quiet.

# 13

I could just about stand, and I thought I was whole, but the trees were moving. The bike lay on its side, and one of Laurie's legs seemed to be under it. He'd bashed a tree with his left shoulder. I moved painfully towards him.

His crash helmet had fallen off, because he never strapped it. I saw that his leg wasn't trapped, and as I advanced he rolled away. His hand darted to the side pocket of his velvet jacket, and his eyes were venomous. I had time to realise that my hands round his waist had been inches from the gun. My legs seemed weak. The gun came free and I kicked wildly for it, getting him on the knee. He howled, and the gun wavered. I kicked again, and this time got the gun. It spun away.

Then he scrambled to his feet, his back against the tree. I slammed a hard right into his guts, and pain raced up my back, then got him behind the ear as he buckled. I lurched sideways, gripping a handful of his jacket for support. He was gasping. I swung a left weakly, and missed, then he lashed across with his foot, getting me behind the knee. It was my bad knee. The image blurred. I saw only his face, and before I went down, before he could trample me, I threw all of my remaining resources into one swinging right, my shoulder behind it, more from chance than balance, and connected with the side of his jaw.

He was going down, so I pinned him to the tree with my left palm. I leaned on him, supporting my flabby knees.

'What did you mean?' I panted. 'Come all this far . . .'

His eyes were stark. 'Nearly there,' he whispered.

'This far from where, blast you?' He might have meant from where he'd left Cowboy.

'England.'

I released him. He collapsed slowly. I stepped sideways, and fell, then crawled for his gun, and found it. I'd had instruction. I'd fired a gun at a police range. I'd never fired one at a human being. I crawled back and pointed it at his head.

'Tell me.' There's always a first. He could see my fury, and believed my intention.

He was dabbing at his face with a dirty handkerchief. He glared angrily above it.

'Tell me.' I clicked off the safety and operated the slide.

'Me an' Cowboy,' he said, his voice slurred. 'It was us at the jeweller's place — '

He stopped. His eyes had gone beyond me, but I'm not that easily deceived. 'Go on with it, damn you.'

He was still looking. I fumbled to my feet and moved round him. Eija's Alfa was parked in the road, and she was examining the score marks we'd made coming in.

'We're here,' I called, and she ran towards us through the trees.

'What's happened?' She darted glances from one to the other of us, looking significantly to the pistol in my hand. 'Are you all right, Owen?'

'I can move.' I jerked the gun at Laurie. 'Say it again.'

He was standing now. He repeated it. Eija nodded. I could see her working it out, but her eyes were on me, assessing the damage.

'Yes,' she said. 'It had to be something like that. Otherwise, why were they both carrying weapons?' She was deeply disturbed. I wondered what I'd missed, but I turned back to Laurie.

'Let's have the rest.'

'What else is there?' he asked sullenly. 'Cowboy said he wanted the lot. He'd felt 'em — the stones — felt the weight of 'em, but she'd taken 'em to Sweden and we didn't

279

know where. Then there was that bit in the papers about the settings, and it said they was all worth a fortune, put 'em together, and Cowboy said it oughta be his, 'cause he'd had his hands on 'em.'

Cowboy, Cowboy! Had he been the leader, then? Certainly it must have been Cowboy who'd slammed the strongroom door. I tried a guess, probing an idea.

'It was you two searched my place?'

'Me 'n Cowboy — yes.'

'How did you know where she was?'

He sneered. 'We was there when he came outa prison. She met him in her little red car.'

'What?'

'All right!' he shouted. 'Ya don't have to listen.'

'Say it.'

'We watched 'em in a café, then they split up. Cowboy lost him, but I tailed her to your place. We reckoned she'd lead us to the lot, and when it was in the papers about the settin's being pinched, then Cowboy said it'd be worth goin' to Sweden, if we had to.'

'It'd be worth that,' I agreed savagely.

'And Cowboy lost her again,' said Laurie in disgust. 'Not a flamin' bit o' good at it. Tailed her, and lost her in the traffic. The goon.' His eyes blurred.

'And?'

'Well — nothin' else left, was there? We searched your place. Mighta bin a letter or somethin' that'd give us a clue, but there wasn't.'

'I ought to shoot you here and now,' I said. 'Then what?'

'Nothin' left but to latch onto you.' He lifted a hand to hold me. 'You know.'

I knew. Cowboy might have been lousy at tailing, so he'd decided to make no more mistakes. They hadn't followed me — they'd been *with* me, and sometimes ahead. I threw the gun away from me angrily. Laurie stirred, but I gestured towards Eija's bag, and he was still.

'We'll have to go,' I told her urgently.

She turned to me. 'Shall we? Where to?' She sounded strange.

'You know very well — '

Laurie was getting to his feet. I turned back to him threateningly, but he shrugged, and stood over the bike, assessing it.

'Eija?' I asked. 'What did you mean?'

She turned and walked away to the car. I followed her, then from the road looked back. Laurie had lifted the bike and was staring morosely at the alignment. I climbed in beside her, and she to-and-froed the car to get round. Then she drove away sedately.

I looked back. Laurie had found the gun, and I cursed myself as he sent a shot in our general direction.

'Drive fast,' I said. 'We can still make it.'

'I'm driving you to the police station at Leksand, and they'll hold you till it's all over.'

'You can't do that.'

'It's all I can think that will stop you.'

'Eija, if I ever asked you for anything, I'm asking now.'

She was silent a moment, and the car was slowing. Then she spoke quite dispassionately.

'Owen, I'm tired of your stupidity. Don't you *see* what's happened?'

'All I can see is that red boat, puttering away across the water. But if you hurry — '

'All you can see is Karin,' she snapped, 'and your damned self-esteem. You're writhing inside because she left you and hasn't explained. Your pride, that is what she's hurt.'

'I'd like to *know*,' I said, 'not listen to arguments. Drive, for God's sake.'

'I could kill you! When you refuse to see what's under your nose, and when you refuse to think about anybody but yourself — '

'Then who must I think about?' I shouted. 'You?'

'Yes, now you mention it. But I really meant Karin.'

Considering that I'd thought of little else during the whole trip, that was quite staggering. I said nothing. I could think of nothing.

'You idiot,' she said, 'that was Cowboy who shut Gunnar Bergh in the strongroom. Cowboy who killed him. Use your imagination, if you've got any. Think what that night must have meant to Karin. There was the frantic drive to find the owner, who'd know the combination, the frustration, the waiting through the hours as her husband's life drifted away . . . She'd have many hours to imagine how he was dying. And Niels, too, crouched in front of that dial, fumbling, and trying to control his panic, with his brother only a foot away behind that steel door. Can you see it, Owen?'

'I see it.'

'And can't you imagine that they'd plan to trap the man who did it, and kill him, somehow, if it took years?'

Not years, I thought, I could never sustain it for years. 'I can understand that,' I mumbled. But something unpleasant was stirring in my stomach.

'But what could they do about it?' she asked. Her speed had mounted. Perhaps she hadn't noticed. Leksand was coming up. 'It had been six years. The stones were not valuable — that had been said in the newspapers. But greed was all they had for the . . . bait? Yes? And with the stealing of the settings — so convenient the sending of them, when Niels Bergh is just coming free — then it was in the news again, and also there was mention of a great value. But to Bergh and Karin there was no hurry for the prize. It could wait. They had waited for six years, and now it is suddenly a great fortune to them. But first . . . there must be the revenge. They could lay the trap. They would lead him in to it, this trap. And they knew it was possible, because he was waiting. Somebody had been watching your bungalow.'

'Been watching,' I said dully.

She nodded, pleased I was attending. She was scrupulously adhering to the speed limit.

'Then they have him, because he would be following Karin if she goes to Sweden. They would see who it is who follows.'

She halted the car, unnecessarily I thought, at a pedestrian crossing. I ground my teeth.

'But he didn't,' I said. 'Follow, I mean.'

'He tried. Cowboy tried, but he lost her in the traffic. You must not forget, there was also the police to worry about. She would have to take some ... avoidance? She must have lost Cowboy, when she had not intended to.'

'So Cowboy lost her,' I said irritably. 'Across the bridge, Eija, then turn right.'

'I know.' She did it. There was now no mention of the police station. I couldn't understand her compliance. There was a strange, quiet confidence about her as she continued:

'Yes, Cowboy lost her, and Niels Bergh eventually realised that nobody was following Karin. It would be a great disappointment, but Niels would think about it. There was something else they could do. They could give their man somebody else to follow.'

I could see what was coming. 'I'm not having this.'

'Then think what happened next, and you will see that you must have it. There was only one other person who could now do the leading, and that was you. So there had to be the phone call. Yes? Did that not fit in?'

I said nothing.

'And what did Karin say?'

I still said nothing.

'Well,' she demanded, not letting it alone, 'what did she ask you when she phoned?'

I opened my mouth, but she plunged on.

'What did she say, when she had left you without a word, and was phoning from Sweden? What was most important to her?'

I knew very well what she meant. It annoyed me that she seemed to have it all put together.

'She checked that a man was still watching the bungalow.'

She nodded. 'That would be Laurie or Cowboy, taking it in turns. But what else did she say?'

'She told me about the snow,' I mumbled. 'Blowing round her ankles. But — '

'But what?'

'But she wasn't happy about what she was doing. I can see that now.'

I believe she sighed. 'Maybe at first she was not. She would think it was leading you into danger, and she still had some feelings for you.'

'Exactly.'

'But later . . . didn't her attitude change?'

'You're slowing. Speed it up, for heaven's sake. And I don't understand what you're getting at, so please just concentrate on the driving.'

'At first,' she said, 'she tried to send you home. But no — you just kept going. Niels would like that, but she was not happy with it.'

'Get on with it. If you must.'

'But imagine how it must have appeared to Bergh. It would seem that *nobody* was following you, Owen. All that trouble, and it had not worked!'

'The police were following.'

'They'd recognise the police. But there was nobody else who could be their target.'

'Laurie and Cowboy!' I said in disgust. She wasn't thinking very clearly now. 'They were there.'

'Well now,' she said in praise, 'you're beginning to see the pattern. They were very clever, you know, your two buskers. They made sure they didn't lose you. They arranged for you to be taking them along with you — they even mentioned heading north themselves, because they'd heard you speak of that to me.'

'On the ferry?'

'Of course.'

'But I picked them up!'

'And did they not carefully arrange that? Think about it. They nearly forced themselves on you. So you offered them a lift, and from then on they stuck to you — or you to them. When they got split up, and Cowboy finished up in Stockholm . . . ' She paused, shuddering. 'To think of him, behind me all the way! But you notice he took your tripod, so that he could reckon you'd hunt *them* out. Buskers are easy to find. And so it went on, and they were always with you, or even ahead. But they would not have been seen as following. Are you understanding what I am saying, Owen?'

I had been, but now she'd lost me. 'I'm damned if I am. All I can see is that you're going too slow, blast it.'

She sighed. It seemed to lift her foot from the throttle.

'Niels Bergh was looking originally for somebody who was following Karin. So . . . who did he see still on the trail, a person who could not have followed her when she came to Sweden, because he was away on a job. The only person who now couldn't be shaken off — '

I couldn't believe she meant it. 'You mean *me*?'

'Of course, you stupid, great idiot. There you were, stubbornly on the trail. Nothing shook you off. You got clues, and you followed them, and as far as Bergh could see, *you were the only one!*' she cried, suddenly furious with me because it was so.

We had forked right, hugging the lake. There were occasional glimpses of it through the trees. What she was saying I could not accept.

'That's ridiculous.'

'Oh, you make me so mad!' she told me, the car doing a little wiggle. 'It's what Niels would see, because he wanted to see something — had to — and there was nothing else possible. But I know you. You're not thinking about him, are you? It's Karin. Always Karin.'

I glanced at her. She was staring fixedly ahead. The car drifted to a halt.

'You've stopped.'

'We've got to get this settled.'

'Give me those bloody keys,' I said angrily, reaching forward. 'You can get out, and I'll drive.'

She closed her hand over mine. 'Owen!'

I sat back, my stomach tense with urgency. 'Then say it. But keep moving, for heaven's sake.'

She let in the clutch again, but her speed was an agony.

'Perhaps your Karin — '

'Not *my* Karin,' I snapped.

'Perhaps Karin would not accept it. As you refuse to, Owen. It would seem to her to be impossible, because she thought she had chosen you as a husband at random.' She said it coldly. 'Anybody would have done for her purpose, anybody reasonably handsome, perhaps, who she could live with and fill in time with . . . '

For the first time I heard her using words bitterly, as a lash. She shocked me. I couldn't respond, but my silences told her all there was, and she went on in a changed tone.

'But because she thought she'd chosen you at random, she wouldn't believe you could be the same man who'd shut her husband in the strongroom. It would be beyond coincidence, Owen. She would have to accept that you'd planned it in that way. Planned it, when the stones had been said to be nearly worthless! But Bergh would tell her that you'd had two years to discover there could be a very big reward for you if you recovered the stones.'

Hadn't I said something like that to Kent? 'Perhaps.'

'To Bergh, that would be the absolute truth. He would have to persuade Karin it was so, because he had to have somebody to kill. She would not be happy to accept that her marriage to you was measured by the worth of the jewels.'

'Worth . . . ' I burst out. 'I'm not going to listen to this!'

'Then what do you think that scene was, last night? Bergh had hammered at her, until she was on the point of believing him. She thought she had chosen you . . . oh, Owen, the trouble you bring on yourself . . . and you managed to persuade her you'd chosen her. That you'd picked *her* up, not the other way round. That you'd picked her out when she came out of prison, and deliberately courted her.'

'But I did!'

'Did what?'

'Pick her out. Courted her, as you bloody well put it.'

'That's what I'm saying!' she screamed. 'Last night you convinced her. This morning they watched you locate the chalet. That was enough for Bergh. The end, because he'd got his proof. He was trying to kill you.'

I watched a sign coming up. Västanvik. 'I'm well aware of that.' Västanvik! Swedish for journey's end?

'Well then! For pity's sake, Owen, they're waiting for you at the chalet. To them, both of them now, you are the man who killed Gunnar Bergh.'

I sat, taking in deep breaths and fighting to untangle the knots in my guts.

'*She* is waiting,' I said. 'Not Bergh.'

'He could be there by now.'

'The speed you've been going — yes. But perhaps he isn't.' I glanced at her, and tried to lighten the general tone. 'But you're not offering to bring your little gun and protect me?' I was intending to imply that the danger was as insignificant as her pistol. She took me literally.

'I do not think I'd dare to meet her, Owen. Not face to face.' Her voice was stiff.

'Then I shall.'

She cried out in disgust. 'But she'll shoot you out of hand.'

'I'll speak to her. Reason with — '

'Owen, listen to me.' Her voice was colourless. The nearside front wheel nearly ran up the grass verge.

'Then for God's sake hurry it up.'

'You came all the way here for one thing. You've said it so often. You had to know why. Well . . . now you know.' She glanced at me. 'You know the answer, don't you?' I nodded. I could no longer argue against it. 'So it is over. It is finished. There cannot be any more.'

So this was why she'd brought me so far, confident that she dared because her argument would cause me to turn back. But there was something else that she didn't see, and there was no point in trying to explain.

'She'll hear what I've got to say, *then* it'll be over.'

It was something Eija could not understand, and she'd really said it herself. Karin and

I had had four years. Whatever Karin had expected, they'd been happy ones. She'd given me so much that I'd hardly been able to contain it all. We'd laughed together, slept together, dreamed together, made love together. And I might have given her very little, apart from my contrary and wild disposition. Yet something had come from it for her — I had to tell myself that — she'd learned to trust me. That distress I'd seen last night had not been pure hatred. She had given me so much, and last night she had watched me throw it back in her face. Or thought she had. Karin, waiting in that chalet, would be suffering torments that I could almost feel, because of what she had come to believe was my deliberate deception.

'All I've got to explain to her,' I said reasonably, 'is that Cowboy was the man they were after — and Niels has already killed him. There's nothing left to destroy.'

She slammed on the brakes. She was sobbing, and probably couldn't see.

'I thought I could talk some sense into you, but you are impossible!' She put her hands to her face and drew a deep, shivering breath. 'If you get out of this car,' she said softly, 'I swear to you, Owen, that I'll shoot you down. I mean that. You could not walk to her with a bullet in your leg, but you'd be alive.'

I looked at her. Her eyes, above her fingers, were swimming with something more than tears. I opened the door and stepped out onto the grass verge. 'Then I could crawl,' I whispered.

Karin's chalet had to be down by the lake. I could see no water to the right, where it should have been. This was holiday villa territory again, but the grounds to them were extensive, and as though jealous of the view they crowded into belts of obscuring trees. Rough sand and gravel drives paced down to the villas. Impatiently, I made a move to explore farther along.

'Owen!'

I looked back. She was standing outside the car, the pistol in her hand. It was pointing to the ground. Her voice held a desperate plea, though it was no more than a whisper.

'*Ei näin, Owen, rakkaani.*'

She brought up the pistol into a two-handed grip. I knew already how accurate she could be with it. I stared into the threat of it, then turned away. I put down my shoulders and began to walk. My calf muscles were trembling and sweat ran between my shoulder blades. A little boy walking, but I was too old and inflexible for a hand to reach out to mine. A bullet was all I could hope for.

There was silence. I did not look back. I broke into a shambling run. The villas to my right were thinning out, and I caught a glimpse of water beyond them.

The last words she had spoken had been in Finnish, and my distress was that I didn't understand. They clattered after me, recurring over and over in my mind.

But now there was a larger open space. The lake was clearly visible, but still the trees along the shore guarded it. I saw white shapes of caravans amongst the trees, and heard the cries of playing children. The sun was behind me, and lay flat on the water. It was a brown, cool sheet.

Västanviksbadet, the sign read over the entrance. A caravan site. I turned inside and ran down between the caravans, towards the water.

There was another jetty, but this one formed one side of a fishing pool. Beside it, an old man and an excited boy were preparing a rowing boat for a fishing trip on the lake. I stood on the planked surface, shading my eyes. The sun slanted in from my right, now, catching dazzling sparkles on the surface, but I could clearly see the black onion dome of Leksand Church, and a little to its left the green fall of grass from the cross with the star. I could not make out the cross itself. The sun seemed to be lifting a mist from the water's surface, and in it I could just see the little red boat. For a moment the chatter of the old man and the child died. They were together in silence, so that the cough and splutter of the outboard motor drifted to me. Bergh was perhaps a quarter of a mile out.

I had to force myself to stand still for valuable seconds. Bergh knew where he was heading, and I did not. I concentrated on his course. It was a little to my left, at a shallow angle. Very little to my left. I ran in that direction.

The boundary of the caravan site was guarded by a high chain-link fence. A group of men were chatting beside a number of pedal-driven catamarans, which they'd drawn up from the water. They looked at me with interest when I leapt clumsily to see beyond a barrier of shrubbery.

I saw new, modern roofs. Karin's chalet had been old. She'd spoken of a turf-roofed outhouse, and these villas were too modern for such things. Savagely, aware now of the approach of Bergh, I turned away and ran back towards the road, slowing as I came to the entrance. There was a cramp in my right leg, and my left knee was trying to collapse against the pain.

Eija's Alfa was parked across the entrance. She stood beside it, stiff and pale, her eyes pleading. She still had the pistol in her hand, but she was no longer tense, but limp with defeat. Without a word she offered the gun to me, butt first. I could do no more than shake my head. For God's sake, I was going to see Karin!

I turned away from her, to my right. Laurie was sitting astride the Honda 750, on the wrong side of the road for Sweden. As I watched, a car swooped past, protesting with his horn. He hadn't retrieved the crash helmet, and his hair was a wind-torn tangle. He looked at me, and when I began to shamble towards the next available entrance drive he let in the clutch. The bike wobbled, and I could hear a grating sound. But he held it into shuddering pace with me, a few yards from my shoulder. In the distance I could hear police sirens. Then they were silent. Another wailed across the water.

It was not a prepared drive, but a narrow track, sloping down away from me, and barely wide enough for a car. As I moved forward it narrowed, and hedges climbed high on both sides. It veered to the right, ahead of me, and despair tugged at my elbow. It seemed to be no more than a walkway to the lake. Yet I had to reach the water, to check on Bergh's approach. Then, around the bend, the hedges on the right thinned. They became a chest-high wall of wild roses, pink and white, and there was a gap in them wide enough for a car. A ranch-style villa blocked my view of the water. A family was eating at a table in the garden. They looked at me, then turned away quickly, politely.

I stumbled on. The necessity to reach the water was now paramount. Twenty yards ahead I saw that the car-width track suddenly narrowed, and became overgrown. I nearly cried out in despair, but then became aware that the high hedge to my left had been hacked away to form an entranceway. Posts leaned from the press of the growth, but there were no gates.

Beyond, there was a lawn of tall, seeding grass, with, in its centre, a single silver birch tree. The other side of the tree, sneaking its shape between the branches, there was a brown, logged shed, its roof turfed with spikey grass. A little to the right of this, and nudging the lakeside trees, there was a low bungalow. It was tiled in red, its walls rough-hewn from pine, and painted the deep red-brown that I'd expected. Its window frames were heavy, painted white, which was peeling, and there were no curtains.

All this I absorbed with one quick glance. It was quiet, but I knew that Karin had to be there, and waiting for me.

But I needed to see the water, and to decide how much time I had. It was imperative. I moved on down the path, which became steeper. Branches tugged at my knees, and a tree pressed down, whipping my face. Then I burst out into the open, with a ten-foot fall at my toes, and a track to my right that skirted the drop. It reached down to a sandy inlet with no jetty, but with a rotting row-boat drawn up onto the shingle.

The red boat was two hundred yards out, its motor faltering. Bergh was paddling frantically with his hands, the tiller tied. Its bow was aimed directly at me.

I think he saw me. His head came up. I ducked down into the branches, and heard a panting breath behind me. I twisted my head. It was Laurie, urgent and wild.

'It's him,' I said.

His mouth twisted, but he said nothing.

'Keep him away from me, Laurie.'

He touched my arm. 'I want y' to know . . . he didn't mean it. Ron didn' know the door'd lock itself.'

Then he flung himself face down in the

undergrowth. I heard the click of his safety-catch going off. There wasn't any more I could say to him, so I stumbled back up the path.

There was a tiny gateway that I hadn't noticed on the way down, and a small gate hanging on its one remaining hinge. I lifted it free of grass, and I was looking at the rear of the chalet. There was still no movement from it. The blue Citroen was parked against the hedge. I walked up to the rear door, which was sideways in a porch no larger than a recess. It had a thumb latch, and I pressed it gently and quietly, so as not to attract a nerve-tensed response. The door was fastened inside. I ran round to the front, the pains now gone, the blood running hot in my veins.

The front door was in a deep porch. There was no latch at all, merely a keyhole. I put my hand to the door, and it swung open. I entered directly into the living room.

She was standing back in the far corner. It was dim inside, yet I could see that there was a table, but no chairs. The place could have been unoccupied for years. I could smell damp and the sour stench of rotting wood. I left the door wide open, to supplement the poor light from the small window.

I had not known what to expect. Not a

hail of bullets, because she'd surely give me time to say a few words. It would take so very few. I'd expected hysteria, perhaps, or a blind hatred. But I'd known she would want me to speak, because she would be crying out for an explanation.

She was standing quietly, settled into the corner so that she could observe every inch of my progress. To her right was the door I'd tried earlier. She was holding a small automatic pistol, such as Sjöberg had described. A tiny thing, meant for wounding but not killing. It had killed once, and I wondered in whose hand. She watched me from behind it, both hands so tangled round it that I could not decide which finger was tight around the trigger.

There was the sound of a distant shot, a shout, then another shot. She did not turn her head.

'So you came.'

'You knew I'd have to.'

The pistol was pointed at the floor between my feet. I stood very still.

'I asked you to go back.' Toneless, lifeless. I almost flinched.

'How could I? We had to speak — face to face.'

'That was one of the ways I knew,' she decided, nodding.

'You wrote: if I love you, to go back.'

Something happened to her face. A nerve ran all down her cheek and drew up a corner of her mouth. There was another shot outside, closer. She did not react to it. I flinched, this time unable to control it, but more at the sight of the collapse of her beauty.

'And did you, Owen?' she asked. 'For four years — did you love me?' The pistol jerked. 'Don't trouble to say anything. You've given me the answer, by coming here. Never once, not once in four years, could I ask you anything that you didn't do. Until now. If you love me!' The cynicism was cutting. 'But nothing stopped you, so how could you love me?' She smiled. The logic was opposed to mine. The nerve response played with her smile and distorted it into a parody. I couldn't explain what the words had meant to me; couldn't even remember my interpretation. She spat at me:

'What should it matter — your love?'

I watched as the fingers went white in her grip.

'Karin, for pity's sake, listen to me!'

'You took my husband's life,' she stated. 'You waited, and you planned to rob us of what he'd paid for.'

Her mouth was a hard line. I heard

302

another shot outside, and a cry of pain.

I held out a hand, palm upwards, supplicating. 'It wasn't me.'

'Liar!' she shouted, and she fired.

I had not thought she would actually do it. The sound of the shot was loud in that small room. I felt a stab in my left upper arm, a blow as from a lashing branch. And then it was warm.

She had lowered the gun a fraction. She blinked, as though feeling the impact more painfully than me. A siren pierced the lake as she slowly raised the barrel again. I forced myself to move forward, but my smile must have been hideous.

To wound, but not to kill.

'He *did* follow me,' I said, but my throat was tight. 'As you planned, he followed, but you didn't see him, because he travelled with me.'

'I do not believe you,' she whispered, and once more I stared into that deadly round hole.

Blood dripped from my fingertips. I licked my lips, and it seemed that I could taste the blood. There were running footsteps outside, but I knew I should not look away from her eyes. The footsteps were ragged, but very close.

'I know now,' I said softly. 'It wasn't for

the necklace, it was for revenge. But the man you wanted — '

There was a crash beyond the rear door, as someone fell into the recess. A shot splintered woodwork, and I spun to face it. The door broke inwards, as I watched, and Bergh trampled in across it.

To move at all must have been taking all his concentration. The one leg was dragging, and blood was now running from a bullet slash along his head above the left ear.

He didn't seem to see me at once. With an effort he dragged himself across the room, to the table beside Karin. Through it all, like a talisman, he had brought my tripod. He placed the pistol down on the table beside a cluster of pallid-looking metal, which must have been the necklace settings, and panted as he fumbled at the rubber plug in the end of the tripod's central tube. It came out, dragging a drift of cotton wool behind it. Then he tilted it.

Like a flow of liquid, catching the paltry light that lurked in the dim room, the stones streamed across the table surface.

He took up the pistol again and turned to me slowly, and I was aware that it was to me he had displayed them.

I knew that I was facing death, more inevitably than from Karin's tiny pistol, and I acknowledged it. There was no fear. Perhaps for most it is that — a calm acceptance, the sudden gift of the withdrawal of imagination. A few might go with a rage at their loss. Many might go in pain. To me it was only the end of a journey. I watched as the pistol levelled at my chest.

'Two seconds,' he said, 'to look at them.'

Laurie coughed from the doorway beside Bergh. He was holding on to the frame with his left hand. He coughed not as a warning, but because he was dying. His eyes told me that. Then he shot Bergh through the chest as he turned. The heavy bullet threw him away from the table and pinned him against the wall. Laurie fired twice more, and Bergh twitched, slowly crumpling. Then Laurie was on his face and his next two shots ran along the floor into the wall. The magazine was empty. I heard one more ineffective click.

Then there was silence.

I turned to face Karin again. The chaos had not brushed against her intent; it was numb to everything but me. She parted her lips as though they'd been stuck together.

'Look at them. You wanted them. Now look.'

Then once again the barrel pointed at my heart. I managed to force my legs to take a pace forward.

'Bergh told you wrong, Karin. Listen to me. Give me a minute. The man you wanted travelled with me. He is dead. Niels killed him on the hillroad to Strängnäs.'

He had killed Cowboy casually and without passion. The anticipated pleasure of it had eluded Bergh in the end.

Karin did not seem to have heard, or she did not care to. Her eyes were blank. I was now close enough to see which finger was white around the trigger. I was now close enough for her not to be able to miss.

'*Stoppa undan pistolen!*' said Eija crisply from behind me.

Karin gave no sign of having heard. Her eyes did not leave mine. I could not spare one word for Eija. I reached forward with one hand, holding back Karin's reflex.

'I came to tell you the truth,' I whispered.

'Murderer,' she said quietly to me, keeping the word between us. I was looking into death when Eija fired.

The gun jolted from Karin's fingers and she gave a little cry, a little cough. I stared at her, my legs gradually giving way beneath me with the release from tension. Her eyes were very open. She tried to say something, and blood blossomed beneath her left breast. Slowly she began to slide down the corner.

I managed to get my left arm round her,

but her weight and my pain bore me down. Her pistol was at my right hand. I reached and took it up and half turned, savage fury racking me.

'Get out!' I screamed at Eija. I levelled the shaking gun at her. 'Get away from me!'

She jolted, as though I'd struck her. She moved a step backwards.

'Wait.' I flung the word, putting all the disgust into it that I could bring up without vomiting. 'Take your bloody sapphires — the lot.'

I gestured with Karin's gun. The stones winked in invitation. Eija came forward with stiff legs. She was not looking at the table. Her eyes were on me. Empty.

I snapped, 'They're what you really wanted.'

She put her pistol on the table and swung her shoulder bag round. She swept the stones and their settings into it, now not glancing at me. In profile, her face was a mask, quite lifeless. She straightened, and in fury, because I dared not allow myself to touch her, I lashed out with the pistol barrel, sending her gun flying across the room.

She turned, and she walked out into the sun-drenched garden. People were shouting out there. I turned my attention to Karin.

Her eyes flickered open. I smiled at her,

spoke softly, my heart lighter because she was seeing me, and the hatred had died, or could not lift its head.

'I married you because I loved you,' I murmured, making her mind reach for the words. 'I loved you because you are you, and not because I knew you had jewels hidden away. I knew nothing about them. Karin, you must believe that.'

I saw something growing in her eyes that I thought was trust. I tried again.

'I wanted you, at first, for my camera. You were my dream as a model.'

The doubt hovered. She tried to speak. Pink foam flecked her lips.

'But, Owen . . . you never did . . . never asked me to model . . . for you.' She coughed, pain creasing her eyes. 'Not once.'

'Because very quickly, darling, I wanted you for me. Not for my camera. Not to share. Never that.'

I bent close because she had to fight for the words. They bubbled out to me.

'It was how I knew. For you . . . always everything had to be . . . for you. How could you have . . . loved me? You did not ask . . . Owen . . . ask me to model for you.'

I clutched her close. 'I loved you,' I said, savagely because she would not believe.

She smiled. 'Liar!' she whispered, and

she was still smiling when Sjöberg took her body from me. I couldn't watch them taking her away.

Kent stood in the doorway. His eyes were haunted. I glanced at the table, and saw that Eija had missed one. A tiny sapphire glinted with malice. I took it up between finger and thumb, and placed it in his palm.

'All yours, Dick . . . you came . . . all there is . . . for you.'

Then I was standing out in the sunlight alone, under the silver birch. My camera was lying in the grass at my feet. I realised that I was still holding Karin's pistol in my hand. I stared at it, not at once registering what I saw.

There was a grey smear of lead along the breech, where Eija's accurate bullet had struck, before glancing off into Karin's chest.

I turned, and flung it high over the trees, and heard it splash into the waters of beautiful Lake Siljan.

# 14

The *Viking Star* edged away from its moorings at Slussen, and turned to manoeuvre its way into the Baltic. The tiny islands were outcrops of naked rock, the passage between them tortuous.

It was June, another June. I stood with my back to the rail, watching through the glass the activity inside the large conference cabin. She was talking to a small group of people, gesturing, smiling. I waited until she had seen me, then turned away quickly to face the breeze, because I didn't want to see her initial reaction.

We were heading out from Stockholm for the Finnish island of Aland. It was to be, for me, a day trip.

Eventually, she came to lean on the rail beside me. She was wearing the same scent. I glanced sideways. She still thrust her face forward into the breeze, as though seeking, with the dark hair fluttering behind her ears. She did not speak. She was wearing a blue skirt and jacket, the same red scarf at her neck, clasped with a medallion over a white shirt. Her flying colours.

'When they'd finished with me,' I said, 'I went back to Stockholm for my car. Lisa Eriksson, your friend at the flat, said she didn't know you. Perhaps you'd told her to say that —'

'No.' Caught by the breeze and almost inaudible.

'Or she thought I looked a poor specimen for you.'

'That, perhaps.'

'I went back to England and saw Kent. He told me you'd been foisted on him —'

'Foisted?' She tasted it.

'Sent to him, against his better judgement. He knew very little about you, only that your languages were useful. I went to the Finnish Consulate in London and they made enquiries for me. They took ages, but then came back with a report that the Finnish police had never employed you. So I came to Scandinavia again, back to Stockholm. Sjöberg had been transferred to Malmo on promotion. I followed him there. He said he remembered you, but he had never spoken to you, except a few words at Hedemora.'

'That's true.'

'Not even in conference?'

'I reported only to Richard Kent.'

'And to your father?'

'To my father, too, on the phone.'

'I went, then, to Helsinki. I saw the Tammela Necklace on exhibition at the Museum of Art Treasures. I asked to speak to the Chief of Security, and then I discovered you'd been telling me the truth. He was your father, Risto Karlsson. He told me you were in Moscow, polishing another accent.'

I did not say that he'd spoken of her with fond pride. She would know how he spoke of her.

'But it takes a long while to obtain a visa for Russia,' I said, noticing her little nod of agreement. 'When I got there, you'd already left. So, knowing by then that you were exactly what you'd claimed to be, I did what I should have done in the first place. I came back to Stockholm, and went to the Vikinglinjen offices. There, they told me you were working this trip to Aland. It was as easy as that. But it all took a long time.'

'You're very good at it, Owen. These quests of yours.'

'There was a question I wanted to put to you.'

'Always there is a question.'

'I didn't seem to be able to find out why the sapphires were so important to you.'

'That is the question?'

'Well . . . no.'

Her laugh was taken by the breeze. 'Then

I'll tell you. It is because they are mine,' she said simply, with a small burst of fierce pride. 'The necklace has been handed down from mother to daughter for over two hundred years. I was the first daughter to lose it.'

'The sapphires were stolen, not lost.'

'But I did not have them, so I had to get them back. My full name is Eija Karlsson-Tammela,' she said. 'With a hyphen.'

'Countess?'

'What? No, of course not.' She was frowning.

'A joke,' I told her. 'It'd take a time to explain.'

She smiled. There was, perhaps, time. 'I had to have them, in any event,' she said, and I guessed she'd reverted to the sapphires. 'There is a legend — a superstition. Sapphires will prevent poverty, betrayal, and wrongful conviction.'

'Worth having around. Especially for the betrayal.'

'They are also reputed to preserve chastity.'

'They didn't help much in Stockholm, and they were useless at Siljansgřden.'

'But I didn't have them, then.'

'You've got them now, though?'

'Exactly. They are only on loan to the Museum.'

I thought about that. 'Diamonds are a

girl's best friend, but sapphires can be a distinct drawback.'

She looked at me, her nose wrinkling. Then she said she ought to be going inside. 'I have a party to look after, a Congress. They are all crime writers.'

I shuddered. I'd had enough of crime. 'There's a way of getting round the evil spell of the sapphires,' I suggested.

She turned to go. I asked her, 'Those last words to me in Finnish, Eija — what did they mean?' I could repeat them now by rote. All through the agony of it, I had clung to them. '*Ei näin, Owen, rakkaani.*' The accent wasn't bad, either.

She looked back. 'I was referring to the way we were parting. I said: not in this way, Owen, please.'

I grinned. Her father had said the last word could be translated as: my love.

'Was that the question?' she asked.

'Eija, you know I've already asked it, *rakkaani.*'

She left me, then. I watched the islands creeping past, seeming to scrape the keel. Presently, she found time to return with her answer.

## McLEAN AT THE GOLDEN OWL
### George Goodchild

Inspector McLean has resigned from Scotland Yard's CID and has opened an office in Wimpole Street. With the help of his able assistant, Tiny, he solves many crimes, including those of kidnapping, murder and poisoning.

## KATE WEATHERBY
### Anne Goring

Derbyshire, 1849: The Hunter family are the arrogant, powerful masters of Clough Grange. Their feuds are sparked by a generation of guilt, despair and ill-fortune. But their passions are awakened by the arrival of nineteen-year-old Kate Weatherby.

## A VENETIAN RECKONING
### Donna Leon

When the body of a prominent international lawyer is found in the carriage of an intercity train, Commissario Guido Brunetti begins to dig deeper into the secret lives of the once great and good.

# A TASTE FOR DEATH
## Peter O'Donnell

Modesty Blaise and Willie Garvin take on impossible odds in the shape of Simon Delicata, the man with a taste for death, and Swordmaster, Wenczel, in a terrifying duel. Finally, in the Sahara desert, the intrepid pair must summon every killing skill to survive.

# SEVEN DAYS FROM MIDNIGHT
## Rona Randall

In the Comet Theatre, London, seven people have good reason for wanting beautiful Maxine Culver out of the way. Each one has reason to fear her blackmail. But whose shadow is it that lurks in the wings, waiting to silence her once and for all?

# QUEEN OF THE ELEPHANTS
## Mark Shand

Mark Shand knows about the ways of elephants, but he is no match for the tiny Parbati Barua, the daughter of India's greatest expert on the Asian elephant, the late Prince of Gauripur, who taught her everything. Shand sought out Parbati to take part in a film about the plight of the wild herds today in north-east India.

## THE DARKENING LEAF
### Caroline Stickland

On storm-tossed Chesil Bank in 1847, the young lovers, Philobeth and Frederick, prevent wreckers mutilating the apparent corpse of a young woman. Discovering she is still alive, Frederick takes her to his grandmother's home. But the rescue is to have violent and far-reaching effects . . .

## A WOMAN'S TOUCH
### Emma Stirling

When Fenn went to stay on her uncle's farm in Africa, the lovely Helena Starr seemed to resent her — especially when Dr Jason Kemp agreed to Fenn helping in his bush hospital. Though it seemed Jason saw Fenn as little more than a child, her feelings for him were those of a woman.

## A DEAD GIVEAWAY
### Various Authors

This book offers the perfect opportunity to sample the skills of five of the finest writers of crime fiction — Clare Curzon, Gillian Linscott, Peter Lovesey, Dorothy Simpson and Margaret Yorke.